Call of the Bear

(Hells Canyon Shifters, Book 1)

T. S. JOYCE

Call of the Bear

ISBN-13: 978-1977755674
ISBN-10: 1977755674
Copyright © 2014, T. S. Joyce
First electronic publication: September 2014

T. S. Joyce
www. tsjoyce.com

NOTE FROM THE AUTHOR:

This book is a work of fiction. The names, characters, places, and incidents are products of the writer's imagination or have been used fictitiously and are not to be construed as real. Any resemblance to persons, living or dead, actual events, locale or organizations is entirely coincidental. The author does not have any control over and does not assume any responsibility for third-party websites or their content.

Published in the United States of America

First digital publication: September 2014
First print publication: September 2017

DEDICATION

For Oscar.

ACKNOWLEDGMENTS

Thank you, Awesome Reader. You have done
more for me and my stories than I can even
explain on this teeny page. You found
my books, and ran with them, and every
share, review, and comment makes release days
so incredibly special to me.

PROLOGUE

Trent Cress jerked his hand away from a rough two-by-four and glared at the growing red dot on his finger. Dillon, that ass, couldn't cut smooth wood if his hide depended on it. The pain was only a minor annoyance as Trent watched the splinter heave from his index finger and lay in the staunched red. Bear shifter healing at its finest. With a quick swipe of his hand across his dusty pants, he snatched a pair of work gloves from the sawmill wall, pulled them on, and hefted three times the number of two-by-fours that a normal human man probably could.

That's what made the lumber yard doable between him, his brother Bronson, and their childhood buddy Dillon. And along with Bron running the construction side of their business, Cress Lumber and Remodeling was becoming downright profitable.

As long as Dillon didn't keep splintering the wood to shreds.

The east wall was made up of garage doors, the ones that slid up and down and were easy to lock up at night. Right now, all three were open to allow that cool Oregon breeze into the mill, so he could see Bron as he strode up the dirt road and past the clunker truck Trent drove up here.

"Shit," he muttered, dropping the wood into the right pile and busying himself with straightening them up. Bron looked pissed, and when his brother was angry, he was a danger to everyone in his path.

And right now, he was barreling down on Trent.

"Guess who I just saw at the bar in town having dinner with Pete Anderson," Bron growled.

Trent kept his eyes wisely at the toe of Bron's roughed up old shit kicker boots. A wise bear didn't look a shifter as dominant as Bron in the eye if he wanted to keep his limbs. Brother or no, the dude was scary when his eyes were all inhuman looking.

"Wanda from third grade?"

Bron canted his head and sighed an impatient

sound. "Reese. Your Reese. She's out with Pete. Why don't you look surprised or pissed or I don't know, anything, Trent? Any kind of emotion from you would work."

"She's not *my* Reese."

"Why not? You've been with her since high school, man. You should've claimed her way before now. She's not going to wait around for you to man up forever. Obviously."

Hot anger flashed up Trent's spine. "You know what? We work fine the way we are. Fuck when we want, go out when we want. If she wants to play around with Pete, fine. She'll be back. She always comes back."

"Why don't you claim her, Trent? Stop messing with her head and make a decision either way. If she's not it for you, then why have you hung onto her so hard, for so long?"

"You want me to claim her, is that what you're pissed about?"

"Claim anyone," Bron barked out. "Anyone will do at this point. We're the last of the Cress line. Did dad not beat it into your head enough when we were kids about how important it is our lineage doesn't stop with us?"

"Claim anyone," Trent gritted out in disgust. "And how did claiming just anyone work out for you, Bron?"

His brother's eyes were so light they should've warned him off of continuing, but screw it. He'd crossed the line. Again. "Muriel was just anyone, and she ate you up and spat you out and now you'll be broken forever. Do you think about her? Do you think about Samantha when you look back on your regrets? She was special, and you tossed her away for tradition."

"Stop it. Don't you say another fuckin' word. She was human."

"Nah," Trent said, spitting into the sawdust at his feet. "Samantha made you *feel* things. That's why you did what you did. Don't come preaching to me about claiming a mate when the ink isn't even dry on your own divorce papers, Bron. When I claim, it'll be for good."

Bron dropped his head and hooked his hands on his hips. "You mean, you won't fail like I have."

Trent scrubbed a hand over his face and felt like grit. Bron had been through hell for six years trying to make things work with a rival alpha's daughter. At eighteen he hadn't had a choice. Things would have been different if Bron had been allowed to pick a mate now, like Trent was allowed to, but he'd been the eldest, in line for alpha, and part of the reason he'd done it was to spare Trent the same fate. He didn't have to say it, but Trent knew the truth of why he'd broken a human's heart all those years ago for a mate he didn't care about. Everything just got so messed up.

"Jesus, man. I'm sorry. I shouldn't be bringing Muriel or Samantha up. I know that probably tears you up—"

"No, brother," Bron said, lifting his lightened gaze. "I don't think about Samantha anymore. Haven't in years. I've let her go. Best you do the same." With that, he spun and strode from the mill. "Don't forget to lock up," he ordered over his shoulder as he disappeared around the truck.

Like Trent needed to be reminded. Dillon was the one who always forgot to lock up, not him.

The sun was setting over the Seven Devils Mountains of Hells Canyon, and Trent stepped out to admire the last rays of light through the pines and firs. If Reese was really out with Pete, maybe she was moving on. A little ember burned in his gut just thinking about them together, but he wasn't ready to settle down. Not until he was sure he wouldn't be shredded like Bron had been. She knew better than to try and make him jealous. He wasn't the type, so maybe she really was interested in finding a mate besides him. A part of him was proud of her for finally believing in her worth enough to move on. He loved her, but was it enough for them to last forever? After watching his parents fall apart, and Bron work so hard with Muriel to fail epically, he wasn't sure.

He'd have to call Reese tonight and give her the okay to move on. She would be worried about him if he didn't acknowledge the valley he'd put between them. Reese was a good woman, who had held on longer than she ought. The kindest thing for him to do would be to cut her loose. Would it be easy? Hell no. He cared about her deeply. But it was fair, and Dad used to say the hardest path in life was usually the right one. It was the only good advice that old badger ever gave, and dammit, he was tired of being on the wrong path.

He pulled down the first garage door and locked

it, then repeated with the other two as his mind swirled around what he would say to Reese on the phone. Stepping through the front door to gather his satchel from the office, he heard a noise, a tiny scraping sound, and froze. Thirty seconds of silence later, he shook his head and rubbed his hand over the hackled fine hairs on the back of his neck. After what happened to Dad, his paranoia had never fully settled.

When he returned to the front, he frowned at the closed door. He could've sworn he left it open. The handle jiggled from the other side.

"Bron?" he asked as alarms went off in his head.

No answer.

The smell of gasoline hit the sensitive lining of his nose and his eyes flew wide. "Bron?" Rushing for the door, he pulled at the handle but it was stuck fast.

His ears perked up at a tiny flick of noise—the rough surface of a match striking the side of a box.

Cursing, he threw his shoulder against the metal front door. The window was too small for him to ever get his shoulders through. The garage doors were locked from the outside, but he tried them next.

The air grew hotter and thicker and flames licked the walls now. He searched frantically for a way out, but they'd built this place to keep thieving rival bears away from the expensive lumber. The walls were reinforced with steel beams.

Smoke billowed through the open space as flames blazed through piles of sawdust and onto the dry two-by-fours, igniting the mill into an inferno. He tried in vain to put out the fire with an old blanket they used to keep wood dry as he coughed and hacked, but it had already spread too far.

Panicked, he gave in to the bellowing beast inside of him. Seconds felt like minutes as his adrenaline fueled the change. The pain of transition was nothing compared to the heat that lapped at his fur as he charged and rammed the thick doors repeatedly, bending them with every pass.

He would kill whoever locked him in here like this.

He would kill everything.

ONE

Samantha Young pressed the wrinkles from her floral dress with her fingertips as she folded into the seat Ryan Cummings held out for her. Maybe if she hid her hands in her lap the entire dinner, he wouldn't notice how badly she was shaking.

She hated this.

Accepting a blind date had sounded like a good idea when she was so lonely she couldn't see straight, but now, looking into the hopeful eyes of a stranger, it all seemed very desperate.

"Margie said you work for PSC," Ryan said with a dashing smile.

Thank God the man seemed to know how to engage in small talk, because she was terrible at it.

11

"I do voiceovers and do the voice work for a character on a cartoon they run for kids in the morning."

Ryan looked around the restaurant, only seeming half-interested in what she said.

She cleared her throat delicately and looked down at her shaking hands. "Riley Reads."

"I'm sorry?" he asked.

"The name of the cartoon I work on is Riley Reads."

"Ah." He tipped his chin like he understood completely and flagged down a waiter with two fingers. "Can I get a whiskey and coke?" he asked as a tall man with a plastered upon smile approached.

"Sure. And for you, ma'am?" the server asked.

"Oh, um..." She searched the menu for inspiration as he rattled off a bunch of alcoholic drinks that didn't sound appetizing on account of they were all made with rum. She hadn't been able to stomach rum since her twenty-first birthday, and gagging like a cat with a hairball in front of Ryan and his pretty smile sounded about as much fun as swan diving into a puddle of magma. Thinking of magma made her throat feel parched. "I'll have water."

Ryan frowned as the server took his leave. "So I take it Riley Reads doesn't rake in the dough for you then."

"What do you mean?"

"You're ordering water."

"So? I like water."

"Should I cancel my drink order?" he asked.

"Do you not have enough money?" She wasn't usually so brash in asking about finances, but he'd started it and she was feeling flustered by his direct way of speaking about things that were none of his damned business.

"I have money, but since you were the one who invited me here, I assumed you were paying for dinner."

Her mouth was hanging open, so she snapped it closed. Maybe this was how dates worked these days. Negotiating who paid for dinner was first on the list of bland conversation. Sure, she'd fully expected to be paying for her own meal, but his too? His overpowering cologne was beginning to smell heavily of bullshit.

A chirping bird song signaled someone calling her cell, but she only paid enough attention to it to turn it to silent, then leaned closer to Ryan. "I didn't invite you. Margie set us up on this date."

"So your job doesn't pay well." A statement, not a question, from Ryan with the pretty smile that was now drooping in a very I-knew-something-was-wrong-with-her fashion. Ass hat.

Her cell phone buzzed against the lip gloss she'd slipped into her purse earlier, rattling like miniature gun fire. Probably Margie calling to check if they were married with a child on the way yet. Patience wasn't her friend's virtue.

"I think it's rude to talk about how much a job pays, but I do decent. I'm still not paying for your dinner though, so by all means, buy all the drinks you think you need to get through this date."

"The price tag is still attached to your dress," he said in a flat tone.

"What?" Samantha twisted in her seat and reached over her shoulder. Sure enough, the red clearance tag that read *$19.99* was still dangling there and had probably been flapping in the wind the entire walk here from her apartment. At least she hadn't paid full price. Her blind date was a douche wagon.

With a firm tug, she pulled the little tag off and glared at Ryan. Her phone rang again, and as rude as she found it for people to take calls at the table, suddenly, that seemed just the way to handle Ryan and his frowny face.

"Hello," she said curtly without looking at the caller ID.

"Sam?" a soft voice asked. "It's Reese."

Samantha hunched away from Ryan and covered her other ear to block out the sound of the restaurant. "Reese? Oh my God, it's been so long." Three years, at least. "Are you okay?"

The woman sniffled. "Trent is dead. We need you."

Shocked, Samantha gripped the gold heart necklace she'd put on for her date tonight. A date that didn't seem important at all anymore. Trent. Trent was dead.

"You said *we* need you. Reese, who's we?"

A beat of silence, then Reese answered. "You know who."

The line went dead and Samantha pulled it from her ear to stare at the screen.

Reese, her childhood friend. Reese, the

chronically optimistic girl who'd always had her back. Reese, the one who Samantha had never seen cry. Now she was crying.

"What happened?" Ryan asked.

"My friend," Samantha explained numbly. "One of my friends from childhood passed away."

"Oh." The server brought their drinks and Ryan slurped down his whiskey and coke and ordered two more. "From childhood, so you haven't seen her in a long time?"

"Him. Trent was a him, and no, I haven't seen him in six years." She hadn't been back to her hometown of Joseph, Oregon in that long? Six years? Her stomach rolled in on itself.

"So, someone you knew a long time ago died. You didn't care enough about him to keep in touch, so what's the big deal?" he mumbled, lifting the menu to cover most of his face. With a put upon sigh, he asked, "Are you going to sulk about this all night?"

"I'm going to go." She stood and shouldered her purse, the one she'd bought to match the dress her blind date didn't deserve.

"Go where?"

"To Oregon."

****

This was a terrible idea. In fact, going back to Joseph was the worst idea Samantha could even think of. She was practically begging to get her heart shredded all over again.

Figuring out Trent's funeral arrangements had taken all of one phone call to her late mother's friend, Sandra. Joseph was a small town and everyone knew everyone. If she didn't hit traffic too badly, she could pull into town just in time for the funeral, stop by the house her mother had left in Samantha's name to make sure it was still standing, then hightail it back to Portland where she belonged.

She was only doing this for Reese.

Not for *him*.

Who was she kidding? Just the thought of Bronson Cress made her heart pound painfully against her ribcage. A mixture of useless hope and deep hurt churned within her until the giant pretzel she'd inhaled at the last gas station threatened to claw its way back up her throat.

She could do this. She wasn't the same girl who'd fled town all those years ago. Now, she was a woman. A strong, independent one with a good job and friends and a life outside of the childhood crush she'd mistaken for true love. She was even dating now. Granted, it had taken her six years to get back out there, and Ryan was a jerk, but hey—at least her date had been memorable. She hadn't even flipped him off when he asked if she was going to pay for his drinks when she left. Another sign she was mature enough to handle a brief encounter with an ex-boyfriend.

The black dress that hugged her curves was a little too tight, but it would have to do. It was the only one in a dark shade she owned. It looked fine when she was standing, but sitting in the car for the six hour trip with a belly full of pretzel had her regretting the decision not to change when she got there.

She was already cutting it close though, so she'd been right to shove herself into the dress at home. She'd even put the extra effort to pull her dark hair back and plump her lips with dark red lipstick. She rarely dressed up like this, but Trent deserved the effort. He'd been a dear friend in another life.

She blasted by the *Joseph, Oregon Population 1,002* sign in her black Jetta and pressed her high heel harder onto the gas. White knuckle gripping the steering wheel, she tossed a little prayer up into the air that she wouldn't be late. Or that the funeral would start a few minutes behind.

When she pulled up to the cemetery, the procession was already parked and the crowd gathered around a hole in the ground. Samantha exhaled long and slow to steady her thundering heart, then slipped a pair of oversized sunglasses over her eyes. Clouds covered the direct sunlight, so it wasn't bright, but she was an easy crier, and since she'd heard the news about Trent yesterday, she couldn't seem to help her emotions.

The clouds were dark and ominous, matching the somber mood of the black suited men and woman in the graveyard. Where her hands had shook like trembling autumn leaves with Ryan, now they were steady, despite the fact that her insides quaked.

Bron should see her strong. He should know that he hadn't broken her all those years ago.

Trent was beloved by the community, and there looked to be more than a hundred people here. The gravel path was uneven as she walked it in her towering heels. Gravestones in a meadow and an occasional pine, and the entire place felt haunted or watched, or perhaps both. And now Trent would be here, his gravestone standing sentinel in the valley before Hells Canyon Wilderness.

Her gaze cut through the crowd and landed on the polished black coffin, suspended above a hole in the ground. Her friend was in there, and suddenly she was bombarded with endless summer memories. Root beer floats at the Cress house, lemonade evenings on the porch at Momma's. Endless treks through the woods around the Seven Devils Mountains. Trent laughing and cutting up, stomping out the serious tones that came with the childhood insecurities of adolescence. She'd left Bron because she had to, but Trent hadn't deserved her silence. The pain slicing through her right now—the guilt—that was on her.

She'd stopped at the edge of the crowd, overburdened and overwhelmed with memories of a home she hadn't allowed herself to think of in so long. Of the friends she'd left behind when her heart had been broken. Of the tragedy of Trent's passing before she got the chance to tell him how much his years of friendship had meant to her growing up.

The preacher spoke up, talking of Trent's honesty

and giving heart—things she already knew, because she had no doubt that Trent as a man was just as caring as Trent the boy. His baritone voice faded to a background hum as she stared wide-eyed at the dark hole under the coffin, waiting to swallow Trent up.

She swallowed hard and bit her bottom lip to hide the emotion that had set it to trembling. A movement pulled her gaze, and she looked up. Bron stood beside Reese, the same and utterly different from her memories of him.

He wasn't the lanky eighteen year old boy she'd left six years ago. Now, he was taller and filled out the black suit he wore until the mass of his arms strained against the fabric. His head was canted as he stared at the coffin, offering her his profile, and the planes of his angled jaw had been shaved smooth. She could see every muscle twitch, every clench of his jaw. His skin was the color of pale cream, and his nut brown hair was cut short on the sides, and stylishly longer on top.

Time had been good to him.

Her breath hitched at her heart's galloping reaction to him. It wasn't because he was still the most handsome creature she'd ever seen, even after all this time. It was the hollow heartbreak he carried in his gaze that he couldn't seem to tear away from his brother's coffin.

She was sad down to her marrow, but Bron had lost the last of his family.

His eyes were cast downward, but even from this angle, they didn't look like the eyes she remembered. Certainly not the same color. When he visited her dreams and memories, they were the icy green she'd grown to love during their childhood. But now...now they looked so light, she couldn't decipher any color at all.

Blinking hard, she squinted. It had to be a trick of the eyes. Perhaps the strange lighting from the oncoming storm reflected oddly against the coffin. A tiny shiver of wrongness trilled up her spine.

The preacher sounded like he was wrapping up, inviting them all to celebrate Trent's life at Bron's house, but she couldn't tear her eyes away from his odd-looking gaze.

His nostrils flared and every muscle in his body seemed to tense, straining against his suit even more. In one smooth motion, he pulled a pair of sunglasses from his pocket and slid them over his eyes. Then slowly, he tilted his chin up until he looked directly at her.

His jaw clenched as he stared at her, unmoving, and the trembling in her hands came back in full force. Clamping her fingers together, she tried to remember how to breathe. He looked so angry, an expression she'd rarely ever seen on him in the years she'd known him. He wouldn't be the same man now though, and from the way he leaned down to whisper something to Reese without ever actually taking his furious gaze from Samantha, she was pretty sure she was an unwelcome guest here.

She hadn't intended to make this harder on him. Her trip here was only to pay her last respects to Trent, and to be here for Reese like she'd said she needed. When Bron finally looked away to the preacher, who'd apparently asked him a question, she swayed as if she'd been physically held by his gaze, and released when he diverted his attention. How could a man have so much power over her still?

A mass of anger, residual hurt, and guilt enveloped her, and she pursed her lips as she debated fleeing. The coffin was being lowered though, and a small line was forming to throw a handful of earth into Trent's grave. She couldn't leave without saying her last goodbye.

The first pit-pat of rain sounded as she scooped dirt and prayed his soul was safe as she released her hold on it. It fanned across the dark wood of the coffin below, and when she looked up, Reese was watching her.

"Hey you," Samantha greeted softly as she approached.

Reese didn't say a word, only pulled her in close and hugged her until her spine cracked. Reese was a lot stronger than she remembered. It wasn't until her friend's shoulders shook that Samantha realized Reese was crying, and with a sigh of helplessness, she hugged her tighter. She'd promised herself she would be strong at Trent's funeral, but the first of the tears she'd been holding back slipped down her cheek as Reese sagged against her.

Thank God she'd thought to don the sunglasses, because when she angled her face, Bron stood a short distance away under a towering fir tree with his hands in his pockets. And once again, he was watching her with that disapproving glare. She turned away from him and snuggled her face into

Reese's soft honey-blonde hair. He could glower all he wanted. Samantha would be gone soon, but for now, she was going to melt into her friend's touch and offer comfort where she could.

"I want to ride with you," Reese whispered.

"Oh, I don't think I'm going to the reception. I can't…" She couldn't be in the house Bron shared with his wife, but how could she possibly say those words out loud and maintain that she was over the man? "My time here will have to be short."

"I can't ride in the car with Bron again and I don't want to be near anyone else right now."

Samantha frowned. "Was Bron mean to you on the way here?"

"No. It's more than that." Reese eased back, and her crystal blue eyes searched Samantha's face. "He's just not good to be around right now."

Samantha slid a glance to Bron, who hadn't moved, and back to Reese. "Okay, how about if I give you a ride and drop you off at the reception?"

"Okay." Reese wiped the moisture from her eyes with a damp looking Kleenex and leaned under Samantha's shoulder as she led her from the cemetery.

The others had dispersed, and when Samantha looked back to the fir tree, Bron had disappeared. Car engines blazed to life on the road and Samantha led Reese to her Jetta. Inside, she waited until Reese was buckled up, then nudged into line with the other funeral goers.

"Were you and Trent still together?" she asked as the soft hum of classical music floated out through the speakers.

Reese was frowning at the stereo dials as she pulled onto East First Street, the main drag in Joseph, behind the red sedan in front of them. "Kind of. I don't know, honestly." She heaved a sigh and stared out the window. "He never wanted to talk about settling down or what we were. I think he was scared or maybe he just didn't see me like that. We were together, but not as serious as I would've liked. I wanted a family with him." Her face crumpled and she shook her head like she was trying to stave off her emotions.

Reese had been in love with him since they were fourteen. A quick tally of the years that had flown by, and Reese had been with Trent for a decade. And she'd just lost the love of her life. Samantha's heart ached for her, and she wished she could take her pain away.

Leaning forward over the steering wheel, Samantha studied the shops as they passed by. Some of them had changed owners over the years, but most were the same. Dress shop, courthouse, diner, furniture store, bookstore and a small mom-and-pop grocery store that was probably still run by Mr. and Mrs. Belleview.

Samantha had moved on and straightened out her life, but this tiny town had remained almost exactly the same. What a strange feeling to be in a place so similar to her memories. By all accounts, it should look different, but perhaps that was the way of small towns. Her moving away hadn't changed anything in the make-up of Joseph. She was only a blip on the radar—a person passing through.

"I can't believe you still listen to elevator music," Reese murmured.

A wave of rain splashed across the windshield, and Samantha turned on the wipers. "Not elevator music. Classical music. And it seems fitting today."

Her phone chirped and Samantha pulled it from the cup holder. "Hello?"

"You have a call from the Benton County Penitentiary. Will you accept the charges?"

Shit. Samantha took a hard right behind the red sedan. She wanted to talk to anyone but her father today. Anyone else on planet earth would do. "No."

"Samantha, your life is in danger," Dad said over the static.

Oh, this should be rich. More psychobabble from that murdering asshole. "Fine," she gritted out. "Make this quick." She refused to call him Dad out loud. That was part of his punishment, because prison wasn't enough.

"I know where you are," he said low.

"Yeah, and where is that?"

"You're back in Joseph and you need to leave. Now."

The car in front of her hit the brakes and she slowed. "Listen, you sick sonofabitch. I don't know how you know where I am, but back the fuck off. I told you, I don't want to talk to you anymore. I don't know how you've missed that message. Stop calling me."

"Sam, they'll kill you."

"Don't call me that." Only friends and loved ones

were allowed to call her by her nickname. He was neither.

"Please listen to—"

She hung up the phone before he could say more and dropped it back into the cup holder like it was on fire. Talking to him always gave her a sick feeling in the pit of her stomach. He'd ruined her life.

"Do you ever go visit him?" Reese asked in a careful tone.

Inhaling a long, steadying breath, Samantha shook her head. "Momma made me once, before she passed. Guilted me into it by saying she wanted her family all together one last time. He calls every few months but that's all the contact I have with him."

"Why did he say someone is going to kill you here, Sam?"

"You heard that?" Maybe her phone volume had been turned up louder than she'd realized. "I don't know. He says lots of scary things. I think he's trying to make me live in fear like he does. Why do you ask?"

"Because of Trent."

"What about Trent?" Samantha asked, daring a look at Reese's pale face.

"Because he was murdered."

TWO

"Murdered?" Samantha blurted out. She wished she could swallow the words back down. They seemed to make Reese pale even more, and Samantha's mind instantly rejected the reasons for Trent being in the ground right now.

"He was…" Reese's voice cracked and she cleared it. In a ragged whisper, she said, "He was burned alive."

"Oh my God. Oh my God!" Samantha yelled as ready tears streamed down her face. She didn't want to imagine it, but horrible visions of Trent screaming and burning filled her mind until it was hard to see the road ahead of her. "Who did this to him?" Her voice was shrill and filled with horror, but so what?

Trent was dead because evil, true evil, existed in the world.

"We don't know."

"What do you mean? The police haven't figured out who did this? You guys don't have any ideas?"

"We have a few we suspect, but it's all speculation right now. None of the...well, none of us ever saw this coming. Maybe we should've."

What did that even mean? How could anyone see something so horrible coming?

No wonder Bron had seemed so furious with her at the funeral. His dad was dead because of her, and now she'd showed up at his brother's funeral to churn up all of the old hurt. She needed to get out of this town as fast as her Jetta could carry her. Her being here was only making it worse on everyone. Her included.

Her mind spun on and on as they passed the road that led to the old Cress house. Bron must live somewhere farther up the mountain now, because the procession didn't even slow when they passed West Alder Street.

Up a winding road they went until the car in front took a left onto a washed-out muddy road. A quarter of a mile more and a log cabin jutted up from the fertile mountain soil. It was all dark stained cedar walls and green shingles on the roof, and the house looked like it was a part of this place instead of some structure man had forced onto it. A long circular drive accommodated half of the cars, and the last half parked in a meadow nearby.

Samantha didn't bother to cut the engine. With a small, heartbroken smile, she squeezed Reese's hand in farewell.

"You came all this way and I want you in there with me," Reese said. "It was always the four of us against the world and now we're down one. I need you and Bron, Sam. Don't go. Not yet."

"He hates me." Samantha's voice came out a wisp of air because her throat was closing up. "I can't go in that house."

"He doesn't hate you. Bron doesn't know what to feel anymore. Or maybe he doesn't know how to feel, I don't know. Please, Sam. For me. I can't stand the thought of seeing everyone's pitying stares, or hearing how sorry they are I lost him."

A single crystalline tear fled to Reese's cheek and Samantha sighed and closed her eyes, defeated.

"Okay."

She wanted so badly to see Bron again. At the same time, she wanted to run away and never lay eyes on him, never let her heart remember what it had been missing all this time. The contrast made her stomach ache. Unsteadily, she walked across the meadow beside Reese.

She couldn't breathe as she crossed the threshold with the other funeral attendees. Now, she could've blamed it on the too tight dress trying to squeeze her lungs from her body, but more accurately, it was Bron's fault.

The man stood, holding the door open and seeming much larger than he actually was in the small entryway. The air felt heavier the second she walked in, and when she moved past him with an apologetic smile, the fine hairs rose on the back of her neck. Something about him made her not want to have him at her back, so she angled her body and waited for Reese to finish greeting some of her friends.

Bron was still wearing sunglasses, but his head followed her in a steady arch as she drew up to the dining room table. Ignoring the hole he was likely boring into her back with his gaze, she picked up a picture of Trent and Bron when they were kids, holding handfuls of worms and covered in mud. Trent's smile was so big and bright, and Bron was gazing down at his little brother with such pride. Stacks of pictures and frames were scattered all across the table and she busied herself with studying each one as Reese talked to a trio of woman across the room.

Some of the photographs had been taken before she left. She was even in a couple. Most of them were from the years she'd lost though, and she watched Trent grow from a boy to a man in those shots. He'd grown up a handsome man with the same dark hair she remembered, and dark eyes so different from his brother's, but his smile was the same goofy grin he'd always carried. She smiled despite her grief at how happy he'd seemed. Maybe her father hadn't ruined his life as thoroughly as she'd thought all these years. It didn't diminish the guilt she carried, but it loosened something subtle inside of her.

As the dining room grew more crowded with people she didn't know, or perhaps just didn't remember from her time here as a child, she stepped into a long hallway lined with more picture frames. These didn't have Trent in them though. They had somber photos of Bron and his wife Meredith or Marian. Something that started with an M. Samantha hadn't paid too close attention when he'd been dumping her for someone she'd never met, and who he didn't even seem to know very well.

The woman was pretty with olive toned skin and dark hair. Her eyes were green and in each picture, she had an attractive smile across her full lips. The more Samantha searched the photos though, the more she realized the smile never reached the woman's eyes. And Bron was serious and somber in every last one.

"What are you doing here?" Bron asked from right behind her. He was so close, his breath tickled her ear and sent a trill of something dangerous through her.

Spinning, she stuttered, "I—I was trying to escape the crowd."

"Not in the hallway, Samantha. What are you doing in Joseph?"

She couldn't read him with his eyes covered. "I'm not talking to you until you take of the sunglasses."

A muscle twitched once in his jaw and he slowly removed the shades. His eye color was lighter than she remembered, but not as creepy as she'd imagined at the funeral. Thank God.

Maybe she was as crazy as her old man.

"I'm sorry about Trent," she whispered.

His shoulders tensed and his eyes blazed. His voice came out gravely and strange sounding when he said, "I asked you a question."

"I'm here for the funeral, obviously. Reese asked me to come."

Jerking his head, Bron glared at Reese's back and shifted his gaze back to Samantha. "When will you be leaving?"

Anger burned its way through her chest. "Whenever I feel like it. I'm not here to cause you trouble, Bron. You're married, I get it. I've moved on, too. I came because one of my oldest friends asked me to. Trent was my friend, and I should be able to come pay my respects to him without you shitting yourself. I'm sorry you lost your brother. Doesn't give you a right to be a dick, Bron."

She sidled around him and he gripped her wrist and spun her. "You left."

"Of course I left," she whispered, daring to let him see the anger and hurt in her gaze. "You broke me."

Ripping her arm from his steely grip, she strode through the living area, determined to put on a proper emotionless facade, but she spied Bron's wife leaning against the countertop in the kitchen, watching her with calculating eyes. Suddenly, the house seemed too small and she sure as sugar wasn't going to play nice with the woman who'd got everything she ever wanted.

She did an about-face and escaped out the back door. Stupid man for dredging up these feelings like black silt from a muddy river bottom. She was almost over him. Had even braved dating and here he was, with his smoldering gaze and that draw that always pulled her to him, and she was feeling for him again.

Stumbling through the yard and to the tree line, she crossed her arms over her chest and sat on a felled log covered with squishy green moss. She'd probably sport a giant stain across her rump when she returned, but right now she was beyond caring.

He wasn't the caring Bron she'd left six years ago. The unfortunate change in him made her heart ache. She'd never met his wife before, and seeing her in person stung in ways she hadn't expected. She was real. Bron had really chosen another over her, and now they lived in that beautiful house together. Hell, maybe they had kids together. Any one of the children she'd seen weaving through the crowd inside could've been theirs.

The truth of it hit her like a wrecking ball. She really had no shot at the life she had dreamed of. How could anyone compare to how she'd felt about him? She'd given her heart to him and he had tossed her away like she was nothing. And now he was angry that she'd come back to her hometown?

She hadn't really known him at all.

Samantha screamed as she jumped off the old bridge near Wrenn Dobbin Ditch. The water was warm as she hit the surface, and she stayed under as long as she could hold her breath, waiting for him. Beside her, Bron slipped into the murky water, surrounded by bubbles illuminated deep blue in the moonlight. They broke the surface together and gasped for air. She laughed and splashed, but Bron had pulled into himself lately and his mouth was still drawn down.

Maybe it was his father's death at the hand of hers

that haunted him. She was shunned by most of the town, and any relief now was found when she and Bron were alone.

"Hey," she said, pressing the palm of her hand against his cheek. "You said you forgave me."

He bobbed as he treaded water. "There's nothing to forgive. I already told you that. You aren't your old man."

"Then what is it?"

He sucked air and went under, and after a few moments, she could feel him swim beneath her and toward a rocky bank that served as a natural seating area just below the surface of the water. Frowning, she watched his pale skin under the surface of the waves as he escaped her questions.

He'd been like this for weeks, ever since his eighteenth birthday. She thought they had recovered after what happened between their parents, but now she wasn't so sure. Perhaps her presence in his life was poison to Bron, killing him slowly and hurting him the more time he spent with her.

She didn't want that. Causing him pain was the last thing she wanted to do.

Slowly, she swam toward him and took a seat on

the rocky ledge beside him. Her bra and panties clung to her body, and she shivered at the desolate look in his eyes as he stared across the river.

He seemed to be choking on words, and his struggle to express himself scared her more than anything. More than the cops busting through the front door in the middle of the night to arrest her dad. More than the agony she'd seen on Bron's face after he found out his father was dead. More than the kids who'd chased her after school and threw rocks at her while screaming she was the get of a murderer.

Words had never been difficult between them until now.

Frightened, she pulled his lips to hers and stroked her tongue against the seam of his mouth until a growl rattled from his throat. These noises used to frighten her, but it was just the way he showed affection. She knew that now.

He gripped her wet tresses and pulled her head back until her neck was exposed, then brushed his lips against the tripping pulse at the base of her throat. So fast she gasped, he pulled her onto the soft beach sand and lay her down. Bron was too large for her to take easily, but that didn't usually matter. He was always gentle and made sure to let her know how much she was adored. He always made sure she was ready for him.

Not tonight though. Tonight desperation tinged his movements. She didn't mind it though because she was just as thirsty for him as he seemed to be for her. Fear drove her as she pulled him closer. Nudging her knees apart, he pulled her panties to the side and slid the head of his cock into her. She was ready, wanting.

"Please," she begged, yearning for the connection with him he'd been withholding.

Gritting his teeth, he pressed into her until she was filled with him and pulled back slowly. Countless intimacies and she still tingled with the newness of feeling his skin against hers. She cried out as he bucked into her again, and clung tighter to his back. Over and over he rammed into her, only to draw back slowly.

"I love you," she whispered, and an agonized sound drew from his lips.

Ramming against her, he set a punishing pace until she could hear the slap of their skin mirroring the waves lapping the sandy river beach.

God, she was so close and his grip was growing tighter as he pressed deeper and deeper inside of her.

"Bron," she cried out as she detonated around him, and hot warmth shot into her as he froze and found his own release.

The snarl in his throat tapered and he dropped his forehead to her shoulder. "I shouldn't have done that."

Shouldn't have done what? Made love to her? They'd been together ten times at least. And she'd wanted him.

"Don't say that," she pleaded, desperate to hold onto the connection she could feel fading between them.

"Sam," he rasped, easing back to look at her. His eyes brimmed with emotion, and agony was etched into every angle of his face. "I'm getting married."

Married. No explanation or anything. She'd asked Trent and Reese when Bron refused to talk to her the next day, but they'd closed up completely and she'd been left on the outside, reeling.

Momma had been trying to sell the house after Dad's psychotic break, and when she couldn't, she started packing anyway. She'd worked at a diner in town, but her boss had fired her after Dad was arrested, and Samantha had seen the way the townspeople treated Momma. Hell, she was treated the same by her peers. They had moved to Portland two weeks later.

Telling Bron he'd broken her was a colossal understatement. She'd been going ninety to nothing through her heartbreak, and hit every brick wall and craggy cliff on the way to total devastation.

She had planned on staying in Joseph with him after Momma moved away. Maybe eventually getting married and having sons who looked like the man she'd loved, but that was stripped away with the three word's he'd uttered the last night they jumped off the old lover's bridge. She'd told him she loved him, while his words hurt like shards of glass thrust through her chest. That pain still existed, she realized, as she hugged her torso in the woods beside the house Bron shared with his wife.

He'd moved on without her, while she was stuck for always in the past.

Damn him.

Through the woods, she could make out the cabin. The back door opened and Reese poked her head out. "Sam?"

It was at this mortifying moment, Samantha

realized she was sobbing like a lunatic. Trent's death and the soul crushing memories that had plagued her were too overwhelming to hold her shit together any longer. And heck no was Reese going to see her blubbering over Bron and his betrayal. She had buried the love of her life today. No way was Samantha going to burden her with her own unresolved issues.

Today was about Trent, not her.

She would just hike around the edge of the tree line where no one could see her, slip into the Jetta and speed off into the sunset. Then she could call and make her apologies to Reese later on, when she was feeling less psychotic.

Emboldened with a plan, she let the tears flow and stripped out of her high heels. Careful to look where she was stepping, she walked deeper into the woods and turned in the direction that would lead back to the front of the house where she'd parked.

Ten times at least, Momma had told her at eighteen she'd been too young to have feelings so deep. She'd called it puppy love and said Samantha would find someone someday who would teach her the difference. Except she was still waiting, and still comparing every man who showed interest to the boy she'd left behind.

Bron had not only broken her, he'd ruined her for every other man.

Her anger grew wider and deeper the closer she got to her car. She couldn't wait to get away from here and work on forgetting all this grit again. She'd done it before and she could do it now because dammit, she was stronger than the ghosts of her past.

A limb snapped behind her and she spun. "Hello?"

Silence filled the woods. Even the birdsong had faded, replaced with the subtle pattering of sprinkling rain on the canopy leaves above. Probably a rabbit or something.

She turned and picked up the pace, using a giant pine tree to balance against as she skirted around a boulder. Another limb broke and she turned, but nothing was there. Panic flared in her chest at the feeling of being followed, and she began jogging as best as the rough terrain would allow her to with bare feet.

Trent had been murdered, the culprit was still at large, and she was traipsing around the woods alone. *Not too bright, Young*, she scolded herself as she searched in vain for the meadow with all of the parked cars. She should've found it by now.

Unless…

Unless she got turned around when she was scared of whatever was behind her.

Okay, if that were the case and she was going the opposite direction, all she had to do was turn around and go back in a straight path. Or as straight as the thick brush would allow her.

As she spun and didn't recognize anything familiar about the forest, her breath seized.

She was definitely lost.

THREE

Four hours of hiking aimlessly and Samantha was beginning to think she would never make it out of the woods near Bron's house alive. At least it was four hours if she was going by the watch she'd fallen and cracked the face of an hour ago.

Sunset terrified her. She was going to have to spend the entire night out here.

The temperature was dropping by the minute, she was wet from the rain and the material of her dress was sticking to her in uncomfortable ways. Her feet were worn raw and when she fell and broke her watch, she also did a bang-up job of scraping the top layer off her knees like the chronic klutz she was. Long legs sounded great in theory, but attach them to a person with little coordination and it was just borderline comical—not sexy.

On the bright side, no more snapping branches had followed her, so she was definitely all alone out here.

On the other hand, not that she was trying to freak herself out or anything, but Hells Canyon Wilderness was known for its bears. Black bears mostly, but there had been several eyewitness accounts of brown bears in the area too. Black, brown, purple or mauve, bears of any size or color were terrifying. The thought of meeting one out here alone was enough to draw a whimper from Samantha's throat.

What was she supposed to do in this situation? She'd watched a few reality television survival shows, but mostly for the cast members' drama. Who didn't enjoy watching skinny girls try to gulp down grubs? The only glaring problem was that she'd flipped channels when the how-to's of fire building bored her. Now, she was probably going to freeze to death out here because she'd decided to watch infomercials about blenders and zombie Chia Pets instead.

Okay, this was where she was supposed to stop

and make up a plan. Sunset was approaching, and she couldn't just go traipsing through the woods all night in the dark. Did she make a shelter? Or should she climb the closest peak and try to build a fire for smoke signals?

The wind picked up, dislodging sprinkles of water from the leaves above and onto her shoulders and hair. She clutched onto the pink multi-tool pocketknife Margie had given her for her birthday last year. She kept it hooked to her keychain and had thought about it exactly zero times since she'd attached it last year. Now, even with such a tiny blade, she felt safer.

She'd started shivering around hour two. A mixture of adrenaline waves and crashes mixed with the cold wind against her rain-dampened skin, and trying to stop shivering now was pointless. Perhaps she'd shake like this for the rest of her life. The end of her life was probably coming soon if her lack of survival skills was anything to go by.

For the hundredth time, she cursed herself for leaving her cell phone in the cup holder of the Jetta. The police force of Joseph probably numbered around five officers, and it could take them weeks to find her carcass in wilderness like this. At least she'd worn her best panties so she didn't have to worry about the autopsy. Sure, the medical examiner would probably find rabbit poop and tree bark in her belly, but her panties looked effin' great.

She grew more discouraged by the minute.

She couldn't die like this. It was humiliating getting lost on the way to the country parking lot in Bron's front yard. No, she was going to be fine. She would make a shelter with her pocket knife and some vines or something and sleep safe and snug, and then in the morning, she'd hike to the top of He Devil if she needed to and scout her position.

Thirty minutes later, she had sawed halfway through a branch of leaves with her useless pocket knife, which was apparently very dull despite her never having used it before. She'd gone to hanging from it like a disgruntled monkey trying to break it when she looked up and Bron was standing leaned against an Alder tree like he'd been there for hours.

She swallowed a shriek and froze, dangling in midair and still bleeding from the knees.

He'd ditched his suit jacket and loosened his tie, but other than that the man didn't seem to have a single dirt smear on him. She wanted to chuck the multi-tool at his smirking face, but it probably wouldn't even break the skin.

"What are you doing?" he asked.

"What does it look like I'm doing? I'm building a shelter."

His dark eyebrows shot up and he pursed his lips like he was stifling a smile. She wondered what those looked like on grown up Bron. "Of course you are. You know you are less than a mile away from my house, don't you?"

"Yes." Shit, a mile? Heat burned up her cheeks like a brushfire. She thought she'd been walking for at least twenty miles. Maybe she'd been going in circles. Primly, she released the stubborn branch and wiped her blistered palms against each other. Clearing her throat, she picked up her shoes, tilted her chin up and marched past him.

"It's that way," he said, pointing in front of him.

"Right. Of course." She spun carefully, heels dangling from her fingers, and walked in the direction he was pointing, all while wishing anyone but Bron had showed up to rescue her. He wasn't exactly knight in shining armor material. More like annoying past coming back to embarrass the hell out of her.

"What are you doing all the way out here, Samantha?" His use of her full name stung. He'd always called her Sam before. Nothing screamed how much their relationship had tanked like formality.

"I was avoiding you. And your wife." Truth be told, and she was a shitty liar. At least he wasn't glaring at her like he had been earlier though, so she decided to throw him a bone of crappy small talk, as only she could muster. "How is she?"

"Hmm. Who?"

"Marybelle...Marilynn?"

"Muriel?"

"That's it. Sorry, I didn't catch her name when you announced..." *Your cheating shithead ways* sounded harsh, even in her mind. "When you announced you were getting married."

"She's fine," he gritted out. She could almost hear his teeth grinding from behind her. "She's happy right where she is."

"Fantastic." Her pride was in the pile of smelly deer pellets on the side of the trail.

"You should leave," he said low.

"What do you think I was trying to do?" She steadied her walking lest he think she was stomping like a petulant child. "I was trying to get to my car but I got lost in Narnia and why the fuck do you live on the side of a mountain? Joseph is the size of a grape. It's about as small town as you can get, and you decided to go mountain man? What happened to you?"

"Nothing you would understand."

She turned and glared. "And nothing you would ever tell me anyway. That's the way you left me. It's your favorite way to handle things, right? You couldn't tell me that you didn't care about me anymore, so you just didn't. You ripped away from me. And now you don't want to have any kind of personal discussion about your life because that would be against your rules."

"Now, now, Samantha. You're beginning to sound bitter."

"Don't patronize me, you smug asshole. I deserve to know why you did what you did. Why you cheated on me—"

"I *never* cheated on you." His eyes blazed and the color looked so strange for just a moment before he dipped his gaze to the forest floor.

"You never cheated, you just fucked me and told me you were getting married to someone else. You had a relationship with Muriel while you had a relationship with me. Call it what you want, Bron, but it's cheating."

"You left," he growled out.

"I couldn't stay and watch you build a life with her. Surely you can see leaving was my only choice if I was ever going to move on."

"And have you moved on?"

"Yes. I'm dating someone." It wasn't a complete lie. "His name is Ryan Cummings and he's an actual decent guy." If one ignored the binge drinking, inappropriateness and lack of manners, it was mostly true.

When Bron lifted his gaze, his eyes looked their normal clear, cold green. An empty smile crooked his lips. "He sounds perfect for you." Pushing past her, he clipped out, "Keep up," and blazed a trail through the thick brush.

She flipped him off behind his back, but for lack of the ability to grow a compass from the palm of her hand, followed the oaf back to the meadow parking lot, where her car was currently the only one left.

"Thanks for not letting me die," she said as she slipped behind the wheel.

He closed the driver's side door and leaned against the frame like he was waiting for her to roll down the window. When she did, he said, "You would've if I let you continue building that shitty shelter. Next time you get lost in someone's back yard, try not to bleed. It brings in the predators."

Like she'd meant to fall and scrape her knees. Narrowing her eyes, she asked, "How long were you following me?"

"An hour. You have a filthy mouth on you."

A tiny screech tore from her throat and she jammed the key in the ignition and twisted until the engine roared to life. Or it would've roared if it were the giant navy pickup truck that sat in front of Bron's cabin, but since it was her faithful Jetta, it sounded more like a pissed off bumble bee instead.

Gripping the steering wheel, she tried to clear her head of the frustration this man caused her. This was the last thing she would ever say to him, and she didn't want to leave bickering. She was mature and strong and he shouldn't think she was so affected by him. "I'm sorry about Trent. He was a good man."

His bright gaze grew empty once again. "You never knew him as a man, so you couldn't know he was a good one." With that, he pushed off of the door frame, stepped back and crossed his arms over his chest as she eased back onto his gravel drive.

His words made her so sad. He stood stoically in the meadow, reflected in her rearview, as his cabin lay dark and lonely looking behind him.

She hadn't wanted to leave her hometown behind, but at the time there hadn't been any other choice.

Not if she was ever going to be okay again.

****

Bron watched Sam's tiny car bump its way down the driveway and closed his eyes against the grief that threatened to drown him. He'd been teetering on the edge with Trent's death, and now she was back home to torture what was left of his soul.

He'd lied to Trent when he'd said he didn't think about her anymore. He'd lied to his brother and it was one of the last things he said to him.

Sam would have been it for him if she wasn't human.

Now, the only mating he'd ever have was the six years he'd suffered through with Muriel. Dad was gone, he couldn't even guess where Mom was, and now Trent...

He swallowed hard and pulled viciously at his tie until it released its strangle hold on his neck.

And now Trent was gone and Sam was back for a night to tease him with what he'd missed out on.

Still beautiful—God she was so beautiful with her dark hair and sexy lips. And that dress she'd worn had probably caught the attention of every red-blooded male at the funeral. Her eyes had always slayed him. Caramel colored and warm, they always lit up with her smile and gave away every emotion. She'd been a ten when they were two love-struck teenagers, but now she was so damned gorgeous it was hard to look away from her.

Everything about that woman spelled trouble.

It was a good thing she was on her way out of town so he could get ahold on some semblance of the empty normalcy of his life now. He'd have to rebuild the mill and pick up extra remodel jobs until the insurance kicked in. He'd thought about waiting a while to start back to work until he didn't feel like his chest was on fire thinking about Trent, but keeping busy was the only thing that would save him.

Inside, his bear was going mad.

****

As tempting as it was to blast out of town and flip off the *Now Leaving Joseph, Oregon* sign on the way out of Hell's Canyon, Samantha couldn't just leave without seeing the house she grew up in.

According to the paperwork in Momma's will, she was the proud owner of the two bedroom cottage on the outskirts of town. She'd tried to sell it, but a murderer had lived there and likely the townspeople thought it haunted. It was hard selling a haunted property that had been abandoned years ago, no matter how low she had dropped the price.

Someday, Samantha was going to use the money she'd been saving to fix up the place and finally sell it. It was the last string she had to cut to free herself from the hell that had enveloped her life here. If she fixed it up nice enough, made it irresistible to a buyer, then she'd be rid of Hells Canyon for good.

There wasn't a plethora of bed and breakfasts or Motel 6s in the sleepy town of around a thousand inhabitants, and if she didn't want to drive the winding mountain passes by car headlight, she was going to have to sleep at the house.

The townspeople might call it haunted, but she knew better. Her murdering father hadn't died and come back an angry phantom. He sat in a jail cell in Benton County, making criminal friends and trading prison tats.

In town, she took a right onto Russell Lane and rode it to the border where the street lights didn't reach.

The last rays of sun had disappeared, and a half moon sat low in the sky. From the crumbling driveway, she could just make out the shape of the old house. The front porch seemed to be sagging, and the roof needed repair, but at least it was still standing. With the run of bad luck she'd had here, she'd half expected it to be burned to ashes on the ground.

The old blue paint was faded and cracked, and wood rot had set in. She pulled a suitcase from the trunk and it made a soft sound as it rolled behind her on the rotten porch. Her key still turned easily though and she sent a little prayer into the universe that no animals had made the house a home in the years it had sat empty.

The lights caught as soon as she flipped the switch. Thanks to the old for sale sign in the front yard, she'd found it important to keep the utilities on and pay the piddly bills every month on the off chance that someone would see this place as the perfect cozy fixer upper.

The hurried frenzy of their last minute move was still evident in the half-filled cardboard boxes covered in old cobwebs that sat haphazardly around the living area. The kitchen wasn't any better, and its counters were covered in light bulbs, unwanted dishes, jars too many to fit in the back of Momma's station wagon and dust. A half inch layer of the white grit covered everything.

She left the suitcase in the living room and hit the tap in the kitchen sink. It sputtered and groaned, and thick brown water finally spewed from it. Thoroughly disgusted, she left it running and turned on the faucets in the bathroom to similar results.

Sadness washed through her, making her feel heavy as she studied the remnants of the home she'd been so happy in before everything went wrong. Her room still boasted pink walls and a wooden rainbow with her name written in cursive letters at the bottom. Her bed had been stripped to the mattress, but the desk she used to do her homework on still sat in the corner. She opened the sticky drawer and pulled out a stack of pictures she'd left behind. They had been too painful to take with her.

The photographs were all of her, Bron, Trent and Reese. Bridge jumping, eating at the diner in town, at parades and festivals. Trent and Bron had fallen asleep by an extra-large pizza box in one and she and Reese had taken pictures of how at peace they looked after devouring so much.

Her lip trembled as she placed the pictures back in their tiny secret grave. She'd intended to leave them here. Maybe this house was haunted after all from the ghosts of her past.

Sagging onto the bed, she squinted at all the cobwebs in the corners and the gathered dust on every surface. At the ruined carpet and peeling wallpaper in the hallway. She shouldn't have let it get to this point. She'd been happy here once, and she'd repaid her home by trying her best to forget about it. This place deserved better than what she'd done. It deserved children swinging on the knotted rope hanging from the old oak out back, and parents discussing bills at the dinner table. At the very least, it deserved to be cleaned up and taken care of.

Her phone chirped and she pulled it from her purse. "Hello?"

"Hey, I was worried about you," Reese said on the other end. "Where did you go?"

Samantha flung herself onto the bed and dust fluffed up around her. With a cough, she said, "I got lost in the woods near Bron's house and he had to come rescue me."

"That's awful. Are you okay?"

"Yeah, I'm fine. Just embarrassed."

"Listen, I was calling because a few of us are going to the bar tonight to celebrate Trent's life. Bron and Dillon put it together, and now Bron's trying to flake out on it, but he would probably come if you did."

"No," she rushed. "I don't want to see him anymore. I think I'm just going to hang out here at the cottage."

"You're at your mom's old place? That thing is a feral cat house."

Huh. So that's what that musty smell was. "Hey,

do you know anyone who works construction? Like a handyman, who can repair plumbing too?" The pipes were still stuttering and she could only imagine what color the water was running now.

"Yeah, I know a couple of guys who could work at a real fair price. You thinking of fixing up the cottage?"

"I'm not a hundred percent sure yet, but I figured I'd get an estimate and then make a decision from there on whether I want to pursue this kind of project right now or not. Maybe if it's just deep cleaning and a few minor repairs it would be worth it to stick around a few days and see it through."

"Yeah. Let me call the guys I know. I can probably get them out for an estimate tomorrow morning since you're on a time crunch."

"You are awesome," Samantha drawled. "How are you holding up?"

Reese sighed into the phone creating a blast of static against Samantha's ear. "I don't want to be alone with my thoughts tonight. Which is why the party in Trent's honor is on the table. I have the day off tomorrow and I'll come by when I wake up. I'll bring some cleaning supplies."

"Oh, you don't have to go to the trouble. I can get them from the grocery store in the morning."

"Let me do this, Sam. It'll give me an excuse to see you again before you blow out of town."

She'd forgotten what a good friend Reese was, and she hadn't realized just how much she'd missed her friendship until now, when everything fit back into place like she'd never left at all. "All right, I'll see you in the morning. Take a shot for me."

"I'll take two. Today sucked. G'night."

"Night."

Samantha hung up the phone and stared at a crack in the ceiling. As hard as this trip had been, and as raw as seeing Bron again made her feel, she was glad Reese had called so that she could try to find peace with what happened here.

Maybe the lack of closure was the reason her heart had stayed tethered to this place.

FOUR

Something was scratching against the inside of the wall.

Samantha would have been terrified if such noises weren't accompanied by the squeaks of a mouse, or perhaps a rat. She wasn't particularly scared of rodents since she'd raised a pair of pet store mice named Chandler and Broccoli when she was a kid, but seeing a wild one would probably bring out her screamier instincts.

The critter was fine, as long as it stayed hidden in the wall near her bed, but every time the scratching and squeaking stopped, Samantha imagined the creature finding its way to her bed and crawling up her pant leg.

Maybe she should've asked Reese if she could stay the night at her house.

By four in the morning, she finally dozed off on top of the bare mattress she'd wiped the dust off of. Curled under her heavy jacket, with a wad of clean clothes as a pillow, it wasn't so bad. And eventually she got used to the musty smell enough to dream of running lost in the woods with bears and giant mice chasing her.

Eight o'clock in the morning tried to burn her with the single ray of sunlight that shot her in the eyelid, and when she groaned and rolled over, she came face to face with Bron.

He was a sexy hallucination.

She blinked hard, but when she opened her eyes, he was still there, crouched down with a troubled look in his eyes and a clipboard in his hand. Her heart pounded as she raked her gaze from his bright eyes to the tensed cords of muscle in his throat, to his biceps and the little curl of ink that peeked out from under the fabric of his sleeve.

Yesterday he'd been all suits and polished shoes, but today he was all tight T-shirts and hole-riddled jeans. She couldn't choose which Bron she liked best.

They were both equally delicious. And angry looking.

"You said you were leaving town," he said in a rich, deep voice.

"What are you doing in my house?"

"What are *you* doing here? It's not exactly fit to sleep in. It smells like cat piss in here."

She sat up so she didn't feel at such a disadvantage. With as much dignity as she could muster wearing a skin squeezing long sleeved sleep shirt and baggy mismatched pajama pants, she lifted her chin and straightened her spine. "I have to sell it, and to do that I have to clean it up. You didn't answer my question."

He shook his head slowly and glared at the clipboard in his hands like it was to blame for the problems of the world. "I went out last night and our girl, Reese, said she had a job for me. Just didn't say who it was for. I figured it out this morning after I'd told her I would do the estimate. I don't think it's a good idea for me to work this project. Thought I should tell you in person though."

Why not? If he was afraid she'd jump his bones the first chance she got, he was sorely mistaken. But he was right. It would be a bad idea. Mainly because she wanted to see him as little as humanly possible while she was here, and having him as head handyman around the house wasn't exactly what she had in mind either. "Okay, do you know anyone else who can work on my house? Someone at a reasonable price? I know it would be giving me over to whoever your competition is, but I'm with you. I think this is a terrible idea."

"Yeah, I don't imagine Ryan Cummings would like that very much."

She was actually impressed he remembered Ryan's name. "Or Muriel." That cat looked like she had claws, and Samantha didn't like to bleed.

An empty smile stretched Bron's face and he stood. "Joseph is too small for competition. No other contractors out here but me and Dillon right now. I'll do an estimate, and if you're fine with the price, I'll have Dillon gather the crew and run the renovation."

For as blandly as he spoke, every muscle seemed to be tense, pressing against his clothing like he was incapable of relaxing. And the air had taken on that heavy quality again, and now smelled like it did after a good rainstorm.

Her voice came out much smaller than she'd

intended when she asked, "Do you need me to do anything?"

"Yeah," he said, standing. "Stay out of the way."

She bolted up and crossed her arms over her bra-less chest. "Why are you so rude to me? The Bron I knew would've never talked to someone like that."

He turned slowly, his eyes smoldering. "The Bron you knew doesn't exist anymore. Don't bring him up again."

"Asshole." The insult slipped out before she could slurp it back in, and now there it was, sitting in the air between them.

He stalked her until the backs of her knees hit the edge of the mattress. Her breath came in short pants as his gaze held hers. He slid his hand around the back of her neck and dipped his lips to the base of her throat, right where he'd learned she was weakest all those years ago.

Her eyes rolled back in her head, and she sighed as she felt his tongue touch the sensitive skin there. When her knees buckled, he threw the clipboard on the bed behind her and caught her waist, then trailed sensual kisses up to her earlobe. It had been so long since a man touched her like this—since *he* had touched her.

It was wrong, she knew it was, but it felt so right to feel again. And right now, as his thumb brushed a trail of fire under her shirt, she couldn't remember the reasons not to want him.

Why wouldn't he just kiss her? She angled her head, but he dodged her lips and slid his fingers into the front elastic of her pants. Her breath sped up as he said, "Tell me to stop."

"I don't want you to," she whispered.

His other arm held her tighter to him, and he slid his palm over her sex. "You're so wet, Samantha. I remember you were always ready when I needed you." His finger teased her opening and she sagged against him. "Beg me."

She shouldn't. There was some reason she shouldn't do this that niggled on the frayed edges of her consciousness, but she couldn't quite reach it. He pressed against her clit and dipped into her once, and she exhaled a shuddering breath. He was waiting for her to ask him, and as much as she wanted to be strong enough to tell him to fuck off, she couldn't resist him when he was like this, offering her the affection she'd missed so deeply.

"Please, Bron."

He plunged into her to his knuckle and a soft growl came from his throat, the same noise of contentment she'd relied on when she was eighteen and their futures had stretched before them like eternity. Now, she could have him as a quick finger fuck in an old rundown house and no more. She would be sad about that later, but for now, she just wanted to get lost in the last moment she was being allowed with him.

Crushing her against his erection, he pressed his finger into her again and again. She was so close. Pressure building, breath ragged, his lips near the tender spot behind her ear.

"Samantha." Damn the formality of her full name on his lips. "You called me an asshole."

She was going to come against his hand and she let out a helpless noise, too far gone to engage in conversation.

He pulled his finger from her slowly as she bucked against his palm.

"Don't forget it," he growled, releasing his hold on her, and leaving the room.

Lurching forward at the absence of his strong

body, she caught herself on the edge of her desk. The one that held all the secret pictures. The cold from where his warmth had been stripped away was uncomfortable and a sob bubbled from her throat. And that was all it took for her to remember why she shouldn't have wanted him to touch her.

"You're married!" she yelled.

A dark chuckle followed Bron down the hallway. Frantic, she lunged for the door and closed it, then leaned her back against it for good measure. He'd ruined everything. Her walls were crashing down and she couldn't deny her attraction to him after what he had drawn from her. He'd known what he was doing, and didn't care that his actions would torture her.

She leaned her head back against the cold wood as a tear slipped down her cheek.

He'd been right. The caring Bron from her childhood was gone.

Bron-the-Man had killed the sweet boy she knew.

****

Fuck, what had he done? Bron ran a hand through his hair as the sound of Sam's crying drifted through the closed door between them. She was shredding him from the inside out, and his bear was roaring for

73

him to go back in there and finish what he'd started. His inner monster was bellowing for him to make her his, more proof that he was losing control over that part of him. He reared back to hit the wall and stopped himself short.

She was human, dammit.

Squatting down, he listened to her sniffles slow and hated himself even more. He'd hurt her. Again.

God, she was so beautiful when she'd given in to him touching her. Head tipped back, wet for him in an instant. She even smelled the same as he remembered. His Sam. Fuck.

He wanted to lick her off of his finger, and what kind of man did that make him? She was in there crying because of him, and he wanted to taste her still.

Trent would be laughing his ass off right now if he saw what Sam was doing to him. He'd never seen the danger in claiming a human and had been loud about his preference for Sam over Muriel. His brother was probably ghost-laughing at him right now.

Heaviness settled across his shoulders and he pressed his forehead against the wall. He wished Trent were here right now. He'd say something clever to Sam and ease her pain. He'd fix everything Bron messed up with a joke and a smile, just like he always had.

He closed his eyes and tried to tamper his emotions. He'd taken Trent's lighthearted outlook on life for granted, and now it was too late to tell him what it had meant to Bron that he was there through everything that had happened.

He was breaking apart.

"Hello?" Reese called from the entryway.

Clearing his throat, Bron straightened. "In here."

Reese appeared in the hallway with her hands full of plastic bags of what smelled like pungent cleaning chemicals. "Where's Sam?" The frown on her delicate face said she knew something was wrong. No doubt her shifter hearing had picked up on the sniffling and hiccupping that was coming from Sam's old room.

"I think she needs you," he said thickly.

"What did you do?"

He leveled her a glare and strode past her toward the kitchen. He'd start the evaluation there, as far away from Sam's room as possible.

Sam had been exactly right about him. He was an asshole.

****

"Fifteen thousand dollars?" Samantha was trying not to yell, but holy moly, fixing up the house was going to drain her entire savings account.

She couldn't even look Bron in the eye after what they'd done earlier and she had busied herself with scrubbing the kitchen counters until the dark Corian shone, but at the actual estimate, she'd stopped what she was doing to gape at him.

"You want me to do a rundown of what needs fixing?"

"Yes. I definitely want to know what that giant sum of money is going to cover."

"Roof needs work, hot water heater needs to be replaced, most of the boards on the outside of the house need to be replaced and the inside and outside will have to be scrubbed and painted." He plopped a page of notes onto the counter and braced his arms against it until his triceps flexed, reading off of it so fast it was hard for her to keep up." New sheetrock where the old has cracked, at least a dozen leaks patched, a pier or two to keep that foundation steady, gutter work, the carpets have to be replaced, an exterminator needs to come out and take care of your rodent problem, and you have a hive of bees in your west wall that will need to be removed. The chimney is unusable until someone can fix the crack running the length of it, and this linoleum floor you have in the kitchen has to go. It's faded and peeling, and kitchens and bathrooms are what will sell this house. I quoted you low in case you'd like to do some of the work—demolition, painting, spackling and the like—on your own. If you want my crew to do it all, it'll add another three grand on top of that."

"No. I'll do it. No more adding money." And thanks a lot, Momma, for gifting her a lemon house. "How long until everything would be finished?"

"If my boys start tomorrow, I think we can get it all done in a week. I'll have to order the water heater, but I can do that today and it'll be here in time if you give us the go ahead."

He seemed so aloof and professional considering the very unprofessional time they'd spent together earlier. She could imagine him speaking so clearly and confidently to anyone he did an estimate for. Bron-the-Man knew business.

"How do I know if this is a good deal if I don't have any way to get a second opinion?" she asked.

But when she looked at Reese, who was cleaning the dusty dining room table, her friend's eyes were wide and she was nodding her head.

"I gave you a fair price. And I'm throwing in the plumbing because I think I know what the problem is and I can fix it myself." Bron straightened his spine and attached the sheet of scribbled notes to his clipboard, then turned to leave. "You let me know when you've made a decision either way. Reese can get you my number."

"Wait," she called. "Yes. My decision is yes I want you to fix this house." She dropped her gaze to the curled corner of the cracked linoleum floor. "This is the last thing holding me here, and I'm ready to let it go."

He sighed, and from his shadow that stretched across the floor toward her, she could see him hook his hands on his hips. He looked more defeated than defensive. "I'll have the boys out here first thing in the morning. For now, this place needs to be a safe working environment for them though, so we need to get it cleaned up and I need to strip this carpet out of here. The animal smell is too strong for my crew."

Granted, there was a hint of cat urine, but it

wasn't that bad. And she'd slept in here all night and hadn't keeled over from the fumes, but so be it. She would spend even more time in the presence of the man who had destroyed her so his pussy crew didn't get their senses of smell offended.

"Fine." She sounded less grateful than she'd intended, but he was already headed back to his truck to pull God knew what from the bed full of tools in back.

"Sam," Reese whispered. "You got a good deal, trust me. He way underquoted you. He won't make any money off this job."

Huh. Samantha frowned out the open door to where Bron's silhouette was rifling through a plastic bin in the back of his truck in the saturated early morning light. He must've wanted her out of Joseph extra fast if he wasn't even going to haggle with her. The thought of his motivations made her insides turn cold. How could he touch her so intimately, and want her gone so badly all at once?

He has a wife, she reminded herself, and another wave of guilt washed over her as she thought about his hand down the front of her pants in the bedroom earlier. She wasn't a home wrecker. The sooner she left him behind, the better.

For the next three hours, she and Reese cleaned the house from top to bottom. Bathroom, kitchen, windows, air filters, ceiling fans, everything. Around hour two, she'd found the old radio she used to listen to when she was doing her homework, and tuned into a local station.

It was hard not to pay attention to Bron as he moved around the house. He never stopped working, only moved from one project to the next. The water ran clear now and the newly cleaned toilet in the single bathroom flushed. The shower even ran, convincing Samantha that Bron had been a plumber in another life. The man had an instinct for it, and he'd even replaced some of the pipes under the sink without even Googling how to do it. He was a little intimidating now as she realized he'd lived a different life than she'd imagined for the past six years.

"Samantha," he called from the living room.

She pulled the oversized yellow cleaning gloves from her arms and blew a strand of damp hair from her forehead. She wasn't even tempted to see what she looked like in the mirror, and Bron didn't deserve her vanity.

"You want the good news or bad first?" he asked as he knelt in the back corner of the main room.

"Lay the bad news on me."

"I was hoping the pad under the carpet was salvageable to give us a little more room with the budget, but it isn't."

"Great." The work hadn't even officially began and they were adding money to the budget. "What's the good news?"

"Look." He lifted the corner of the carpet and pulled the blue speckled pad up along with it. Underneath were dirty wooden planks. "You have wood floors under these carpets. I bet I can sand and re-stain them, and it'll be another good selling point for the house. We won't have to pay for new carpet in here either."

"Really?" She loved wood floors. Grabbing the corner, she pulled backward with all of her mite, and it budged an estimated three inches. Stupid scrawny arms.

The corner of Bron's sexy lip turned up and he nodded his head for her to back up. Then with one stout yank, he pulled it to the middle of the room and went to work on another corner.

"I loosened it," she muttered.

He barked a laugh but it couldn't be at her. He was too far away to hear over the blaring radio crooning about a couple finding their luck someday. Still, she was thankful for whatever had amused him, because it had been so long since she'd heard that booming laugh of his. She would never admit it, but it was the sound she'd missed the most, and it warmed the places in her that had gone cold with his distance. Even if the laugh wasn't for her, she was going to cherish it.

With the old musty carpet removed and tossed onto the overgrown front lawn, the house seemed bigger and already smelled much better.

"I'm hungry," she said as Reese came out of Momma's old bedroom with an armful of linens they'd left behind. "You want to go to the cafe in town? My treat for helping me with all of this. Really, I owe you about thirty lunches."

"You don't owe me anything. Today has been a beautiful distraction from the crap that's been going on," Reese said with a sad smile. "I didn't have any plans this morning and sitting around won't do me any favors. Besides, I missed you. It's been nice spending time with you, even if it's just cleaning. We spent a lot of hours in this house together."

"Momma always joked she might as well adopt you, you slept over so much." Memories of inseparable summers brought a smile to her face. "I'm still hungry."

Reese dropped the linens onto the wooden floorboards and wiped her hands. "Come on, Young. It's probably been way too long since you had a good chicken fried steak."

Locking up wouldn't matter. If no one had robbed the place or squatted here before now, it was a pretty safe bet they wouldn't pick tonight to do so. Plus it was a small town. That's just what people did—left their doors unlocked.

She turned, determined to invite Bron to lunch in a very civilized manner, but he was pulling at the back of his shirt and it was over his head before she could say a word. His skin had always been the color of cream, so fair he practically glowed, but across his upper arm was a tribal tattoo of some kind. And Bron's lanky days long behind him, now he was all man with muscles that rippled across his arms and stomach as he reached for a clean shirt. From his profile, the sun hit every abdominal muscle, and his jeans hung so low, she followed the flexed crease that bracketed his hip and delved into the waist of his pants.

"Holy. Shit," she muttered.

Bron's gaze jerked to her and he froze.

"Nice and subtle," Reese drawled, shaking her head beside Samantha.

Heat seared up her neck and landed in her cheeks as he gave her a calculating look and pulled the other shirt over his head. She'd known he was well built from the way he filled out the suit yesterday, and from the way his arms pressed against the threadbare fabric of his work shirt today. But this was ridiculous. He was perfectly chiseled like some MMA fighter or something. She didn't remember Bron being a gym rat, but maybe it was yet another thing she just didn't know about him anymore.

"You should see your face right now," Reese said with a knowing smile. "You look like you just ovulated."

Ignoring Reese, Samantha called, "You want to go to lunch with us?" Her voice sounded airy and desperate. "I mean, we're going anyway, and I feel like the least I can do for you fixing the plumbing is buy you a meal."

"No," he clipped out.

She narrowed her eyes at his stern tone.

"No, thank you," he corrected himself with a grim set to his mouth. "I'm going to go make some calls. The boys will be out here in the morning. You ladies have a nice day." With that, he walked around his truck and hopped into the driver's seat. The engine roared to life and he sped off like he couldn't get away from her fast enough.

She watched his pickup disappear around the corner. It had been stupid to invite him. She glared at the stained carpet draped across the weedy front yard and blamed her psychotic break on the cat piss fumes.

FIVE

"Give me your phone," Reese said.

"Hmm?" Samantha asked, dragging her gaze from the large picture window in the front of the cafe. She could've sworn the couple making out on the park bench outside used to sit near in her science class. She just couldn't remember their names.

"Phone." Reese waved her hand impatiently. "You'll need Bron's number in case anything comes up at the house."

Suspiciously, Samantha narrowed her eyes as she handed it over. "Why do I get the feeling you are pushing us together? Why didn't you tell me the guy you knew for construction work was Bron and his crew? You could've just said that yesterday."

"Would you have okayed him to come over and look at the house?"

"No."

"That's why I didn't tell you. You would've been on East First Street headed out of town by dawn this morning if you knew he was your only option at rehabbing your house. I want you to stay."

"Reese, I'm not staying. You heard Bron when he said the job will only take a week. Already the place is looking better. This is just temporary. I have a life back in Portland."

"Even if you're here for a week, it's better than a day," Reese said softly as she hit save on the number she'd entered and handed the phone back.

"Why did we stop talking?" Samantha asked suddenly. There hadn't ever been a big blow-out fight or anything. The phone calls had just gone longer and longer in between.

"Life happened," Reese said with a shrug. "You were busy, I was busy, we didn't ever see each other and neither one of us was ever big on phone talk when we were kids. We'd always just ride our bikes over to each other's house and hang out."

"Well, I'm sorry I didn't make more of an effort. I

should've kept in touch with Trent too, but with him, I was scared he still hated me after what my dad did."

"Sam, I can't tell you why right now, but I will say that Trent wasn't mad at what your father did. Neither was Bron." She lowered her voice and leaned forward. "He had his reasons for doing what he did, and the Cress boys understood that."

Frowning so hard it hurt her face, she asked, "What do you mean?" She sure didn't understand Dad's reasons for stalking Mr. Cress in the middle of the night and knifing him to death in the woods behind his house, so how had his sons forgiven so easily?

"Nothing. Forget I said anything." Reese smiled at the waitress and rattled off her order like a pro.

Samantha's mental facilities had shut down completely, so she murmured, "I'll have the same," and hoped Reese hadn't ordered anything with jalapenos.

"Reese, what's going on?" she asked as the waitress bustled away. "Do you know something about what happened with my dad that I don't?"

"No. Forget it. I'm serious. Look, if you stick around long enough, you'll figure it all out. A week isn't going to be enough time though, I'm telling you that right now. Stay in Joseph and give this place another chance."

"Reese," she groaned, lobbing her head back and staring at the ceiling tiles. Lowering her chin again, she said, "I can't stay here for the same reasons I left. Bron...shit." She clenched and unclenched her hands to steady their traitorous shaking. "I can't watch him and his wife flitting around town holding hands and making googly eyes at each other. I'm not that strong." Yet. She wasn't that strong *yet*.

Reese nearly choked on the cola she was slurping. "Who, Muriel?"

"Yes, Muriel. Or is there another wife I should be concerned with?"

"Have you asked Bron about his wife?" Reese said the last word like it was a curse.

"It's not exactly appropriate conversation to have with him considering our past history. No, I'm not asking him about the woman he left me for."

"Well," Reese muttered, stirring her straw around the dark, bubbly fountain drink. "I think you should." Silence stretched between them, and finally she said, "You should come out to Bron's house tonight at seven. Maybe it'll answer some of the questions you have."

"Why would I go anywhere near his house? He borderline hates me, and I don't feel like getting shot for trespassing. Plus I was just lost in the woods there yesterday. I'm still traumatized from my last near death experience."

"Suit yourself." Reese lifted her sky blue gaze to hers and canted her head. "But you might learn why Bron is the way he is now."

More freaking mysteries from Reese and she was beginning to sound like one of those palm readers who threw out just enough information to keep the client hooked. Samantha wasn't playing unravel-the-mysteries-around-Bron. The more she knew about him, the more he hurt her, and the more she wanted him despite it all. And that was a deadly combination to her already weary heart.

Over her cold, dead, lifeless, rigor mortised body would she be popping over to his cabin unannounced tonight.

****

Samantha was definitely hiking through the woods again, just a day after being lost in them the first time, only this time, she was doing it in the dark. At least she had a flashlight, like a freaking sleuth on a mission.

Jesus, she was going to get shot. The good people of Joseph were open gun carriers, and Bron seemed the type to know his weapons. She'd seen the shotgun he had on a rack in the back window of his truck.

Reese, that little poop stirrer, had given just enough enticing bread crumbs of information to make her go crazy the rest of the day, and at the last minute, she'd hopped in her car and parked it on the road before Bron's driveway. Just like Reese said to. Why was she getting the feeling she should have strings attached to her limbs so Reese could play puppeteer easier?

Why did she always get herself into these situations? Why couldn't she just leave well enough alone? Bron was happy with Muriel, while she was playing Stalker, Stalker in the Woods. She was probably going to jail tonight. Maybe Dad could give her tips on picking the right prison gang.

Light shone through the trees up ahead, and she could make out the meadow she'd parked in yesterday. The porch lights of Bron's cabin lit up the entire clearing, and in front of the house at least fifty townspeople were gathered. A town meeting at dark, and she hadn't seen a single flyer on the light poles on East First announcing it. What kind of weird neighborhood watch shit was this?

A vaguely familiar man stood on the porch stairs talking too low for her to hear from this distance.

She clicked off the flashlight and took a wide loop through the trees to get closer until she couldn't move without being seen. Belly crawling sounded awesome in theory, but in reality, it was loud and there were sharp sticks and rocks that booby-trapped the ground and poked her in the stomach. Her ascent was slow and terribly clumsy, but at least she wiggled close enough to the tree line to catch some of what the tall man was saying.

"I think right now, we have to consider that the threat could be coming from anywhere," he said. His hair shone raven black with streaks of silver in the light of the house, and his eyes looked dark to match them. His jaw was stubbled with glints of gray, and he wore a leather motorcycle jacket and fitted jeans over heavy black boots.

Beside him, Bron rocked slowly in a chair with his

hands clasped in front of his face. He shook his head. "You know it's probably the Marsdens who did this to Trent. It's on me."

A murmur rippled through the crowd and the tall man trilled a sharp whistle. They quieted immediately. "You think this is a revenge killing, Cress? Your pairing with Muriel failed, so her daddy killed your brother? What would that gain for his clan? War, that's what, and they're outnumbered. That old bruiser doesn't have the nuts to pull this off. Not in broad daylight. Not in our territory."

"Then who?" someone asked from the crowd. "Marsden is the only one who sounds right for this."

"The possibility exists that this could be a resurgence of hunters, or someone caught wind of Trent in town and took it upon themselves to kill what scared them."

What in the actual fuck were they talking about? She looked from profile to profile, and none of them seemed surprised by the turn of conversation, or at the easy way this man talked about Trent's death. Like this was every day chit-chat, and a murder hadn't just occurred.

The breeze drafted up her back and lifted a

strand of hair that had fallen out of her bun. Bron's reaction was instantaneous. His nostrils flared and he jerked his gaze directly to her. Shit.

Pursing his lips, he shook his head slightly. Yeah, she got it—she shouldn't get caught spying on the cult meeting. Freaking Reese for getting her here. Now Samantha was too terrified to move, and she needed to escape this place as soon as humanly possible.

A man on the edge of the crowd twitched his head in her direction and frowned.

Crap, crap, crap.

After a few moments, he turned his attention back to a question that had been asked from one of the townspeople.

Her terrified grasp loosened on a thatch of wild grass.

"Hunters are being eyed for this because I got a call from Tommy Young yesterday," the tall biker said.

Her body jerked at the mention of Dad's name and the dry leaves under her crackled. Dad put a phone call in to Leather Jacket? Why?

"I move we reschedule this meeting to tomorrow

night," Bron rushed, standing.

"What? No," Leather Jacket said. "We're all here now. Let's discuss how we're going to handle the old—"

A stony hand clamped onto her shoulder and Samantha screamed in shock as the man from the edge of the crowd dragged her upward. His grip hurt, and she imagined his fingers digging all the way to her bones.

The man lurched back and was slammed onto the ground, and the absence of his punishing grip made her stumble forward.

Bron had his hand around the man's throat, and a feral sound ripped from both of them. Samantha stared dumbly from the rocking chair, still swaying, to the twenty yard distance Bron had crossed in a second's time. It wasn't possible. It wasn't physically possible for him to move that fast.

"Bronson," Leather Jacket barked out.

The clearing stilled and not even the night critters in the woods behind her dared to chirp. The air smelled funny, electric, and Bron stood slowly, blocking her view completely with the wide planes of his back.

Rubbing her throbbing shoulder, she tried to peek around him, but he moved in front of her again.

The man on the ground looked furious, if the mauve color of his face was anything to go by, but he rose and headed back to the onlookers, whose eyes all seemed to be riveted to her and Bron.

"Who is she?" Leather Jacket asked in a booming voice.

"She's no one."

"Is she yours?" the man asked in a careful tone.

His? She wasn't anyone's, and she definitely didn't belong to some two-timing back-stabbing liar. Oh, she'd heard loud and clear when they were discussing Bron's failed marriage. His refusal to enlighten her earlier was as good as a lie in her book.

Bron still hadn't answered, so she spoke up. "I'm not his anything. Well, I'm his client. He's working on my house for me and I…had a question about the plumbing. And the…cat pee. And the water meter."

Bron's irritated sigh turned into a soft rumble in his chest. "That's water *heater*, and they can tell you're lying. You're terrible at it. And what are you wearing?"

She looked down at her skin tight black ensemble.

"Black Lycra." For spying better, clearly.

"Jesus," he muttered.

"What's your name?" Leather Jacket asked in a soft voice that was seriously starting to scare her.

"Samantha."

He sniffed a humorless laugh and rocked his head back. "Let me guess. Samantha Young."

The crowd surged toward her. Angry yells and crude names filled the night air and Bron's arm snaked around her waist. "She's mine, she's mine. She's mine!"

"What are you—"

"Shhh," he hissed.

Well, that was just rude. She didn't understand anything. These people knew Dad, knew her, even though she only recognized a few faces in the crowd. Reese was one of them, and her friend looked terrified.

"You know what she is," Leather Jacket said in an angry rumble.

"Yes." Bron's profile grew rigid as he watched the man, and the muscles in his jaw danced as he clenched his teeth.

"Your place here will be compromised, do you

understand what I'm saying to you?"

Bron's chest heaved, and he whispered, "Fuck," and dropped his gaze to Samantha's.

"What's happening?" she asked in a tiny voice. The mob looked ready to kill her, and Dad's warning over the phone suddenly frightened her. Maybe she should've taken him more seriously, because she obviously had no idea what was going on in the shadowy underbelly of Joseph.

"It's going to be okay," he whispered. But the cool, stony look in his eyes said he hated her in this moment. Pulling his gaze back to the man, he said, "I understand."

"No!" Reese yelled. "Dodger, this isn't how it's supposed to happen."

"Did you know she came back?" the man, Dodger, asked Reese. His face was morphing into something fearsome. "And you didn't tell me? Tread carefully, or your fate will be the same as his."

Reese's lip trembled and her eyes filled with moisture as she dropped her chin to her chest. "But he's a Cress."

"Tradition or no, he has to abide by the same rules the rest of us do." The authority in his voice cracked across the clearing.

"I don't understand." Samantha couldn't pull her eyes away from the tear that stained Reese's cheek. She'd done something bad. She could feel it, and from the somber faces in the crowd, they hadn't wanted whatever judgment that cult leader, Dodger, was handing out either.

She shouldn't have come.

"I'm taking her home. Stay as long as you need to," Bron said to the towering man on the porch. Without a word of warning, he grabbed her hand and dragged her toward the crowd. He cut a straight path through the people gathered on his lawn, but someone wrapped their fingers in Samantha's hair and ripped her backward.

She gasped in pain, and Bron turned so fast he blurred. He gripped a woman's wrist and growled, "Let her go, or so help me, I'll fuckin' kill you. I have nothing else to lose."

Samantha's heart was in her throat, pounding so hard it was impossible to breathe. She could feel the strands of her hair separating from her scalp in the woman's grip, but it loosened and she shoved Samantha's head forward. Bron angled his face in a silent warning, never letting his gaze drop from the woman's. His eyes were blazing, and his lips pursed in a thin line—a look of fury she'd never seen on his face before.

Turning, he pulled her behind him and led her to his truck. Throwing open the passenger side door, he hefted her into the seat like she weighed nothing and pulled the buckle over her lap like she was incompetent. Slamming the door, he strode around the front of the truck with long, lithe strides and slid in behind the wheel.

The truck rocked with the force of his door shutting.

"What the hell was that?" she asked breathily.

"Stop. Talking," he gritted out through his clenched teeth.

"Why do you think you can talk to me like that?"

He turned the key and revved the engine. "They can still hear you."

How? The others were ten yards away from the truck at least, and she'd been whispering.

"Fine. You let me know when you feel like having a civil conversation that doesn't end with you talking down to me." She twisted the radio volume and he hunched into himself when a country song blared through the speakers.

"Dammit, woman." Bron hit the volume button once and the noise died to nothing. "You're killing my patience and my ear drums. Just sit still until I get us out of here."

What Dodger had said rattled around in her mind as Bron pulled around the yard and onto his gravel drive. Her dad was involved with what they were doing up here, but how? He was in prison. And how could hunters be to blame if Trent was burned alive? Hunting accidents happened in Hells Canyon, but as far as she knew, never by fire. It was always a wayward bullet that hit an unsuspecting target.

"Bron, who is that man?"

"He's the boss around here, and that's all you need to know."

"No, that's not all I need to know. He said my dad's name. What does my dad have to do with any of this? Does he think he was the one who killed Trent?"

"No, not him. The people he works with. Have you talked to your dad about what happened?"

"I can count the number of conversations I've had with him on one hand. The man is certifiable. He called me yesterday and said I need to leave here or someone will kill me."

Bron ripped his gaze away from the road long enough to give her a wide-eyed glance. "Tell me exactly what he said, word for word."

She repeated their brief conversation as best she could.

"Shit. Does he mean you'll be killed by my people or his?"

Samantha pressed her cool palms against her cheek and inhaled deeply, then leaned back against the seat. "You're scaring me. I don't know what any of this means. His people or your people. What are you saying?"

He licked his lips and shook his head. "I can't tell you any more than I already have. If you want to know more, answer your dad's phone calls."

"Answer my…" A haunting realization brushed over her. "Have you been talking to him?"

"To who?"

"My dad. And I swear if you lie to me, I'll never forgive you."

Clamping his mouth shut, Bron stared at the dirt road in his high beams.

With a humorless laugh, she nodded and looked out her window. Of course he had. Because not talking to the man who was currently serving ten years for murdering his father would make sense. And nothing about this town made any damned sense anymore.

This felt like a betrayal, the two men who'd hurt her the most talking behind her back.

"What did you mean when you said I was yours?"

"Doesn't matter because it won't stick. You need to get out of here. Everything will go back to normal when you're gone."

"I'm not leaving here confused like I did the last time. I can't move on like that if I'm always questioning everything. Surely you can see that isn't an option. For six years, I've circled around the reasons why you did what you did, and now I'm even more confused. And why didn't you tell me about Muriel? You said she was happy."

"She is happy. She isn't with me anymore, so she's probably happier than she's ever been." His eyes had a strange glow that reflected off the window, and he refused to look at her.

"Did you love her?"

"No."

Her lip trembled and she bit it. Hard. "Then why did you leave me for her?"

His chest heaved and the cab of his truck felt too small. She couldn't breathe and the longer he went without answering, the more she was sure he wouldn't. At a stop sign at the road, she shoved the door open and stumbled out before he'd even come to a complete stop.

"Samantha, what are you doing?"

"What I'm not doing is running around in circles while you get in my head and confuse the hell out of me again, Bronson." Yeah, full name. If he was going to insist on formality with her name, she was doing it back. Dick move battle. She hoped it hurt him like it hurt her.

"Are you in trouble?" she asked.

"What do you mean?" he demanded, arm still draped over his steering wheel and glaring at her through the open passenger side door.

"I mean, are you in a cult or something. Is that what I saw back there? Some secret society that hurts outsiders. Because they were going to hurt me, weren't they? That's why you said I was yours. It wasn't because you actually care about me, Bronson. I'm not stupid, nor am I clinging to the hope that the man I cared for will come back to me someday. I'm a realist. You don't know how to feel for me like I deserve. You said I was yours because you don't want my blood on your hands."

"What do you want from me?"

Her insides were breaking apart. What did she want from him? Everything. No one would ever, could ever, feel about him the way she had, and he'd tossed her away like she was nothing. "I want you to finish my house. I want you to stop talking to me, and just treat me like any other client. And when the job is done, I want you to take my money, and shake my hand like we don't know each other, and then I don't want to ever hear from you again."

She turned and strode for her car, dark and shiny under the moonlight.

The buzz of his automatic windows sounded and he pulled up beside her. "Why were you at my house tonight, Samantha? Why now?"

"Reese told me to be here."

A curse left Bron's lips. "Wait," he drawled.

She pulled the handle of her Jetta and sank into

the driver's seat, then slammed the door beside her.

Most of her life had been spent *waiting* on Bron.

Most of a lifetime was long enough.

SIX

A pounding knock rattled the house and Samantha squinted her eyes open. It was barely light out.

With a groan, she rolled out of bed and stumbled to the front door. Throwing it open, she narrowed her eyes at the three men standing in front of her house. One looked like an older version of Dillon Tanner who used to sit next to her in English class, one was a complete stranger who was roughly the size of a Clydesdale horse, and the last was Bron, who looked tired and ruffled and was frowning at her legs.

Dillon whistled a catcall and Bron shoved his way past his crew, plucked her off her feet like she weighed little more than a kitten, and barreled back down the hallway toward her room.

"Let go of me!" she yelped.

"Then wear some damned pants when you answer the door."

Mortified, she squeezed her eyes closed, then dared a glance at her lacy red underwear. She went to bed with pants on, but sometimes she kicked out of them if she got too hot in her sleep. And the window unit in her room was definitely still capable of blasting out some serious heat.

"Well, I wasn't all the way awake yet on account of the moon still being out."

"Be serious," he said, tossing her onto the bed. "It's six, and I told you we'd be here first thing in the morning."

"No, you said your crew would. What are *you* doing here, Bron?"

He hooked his hands on his waist and lifted his brows like she was being unreasonable. "I'm trying to get you out of town as soon as possible. That's why I'm here."

He was staring at her panties.

Jerking the covers over her indecent half, she glowered. "You look tired."

"I slept in my truck."

"Did Muriel get the house in the divorce you failed to mention?"

He lifted his chin and the look he gave her was nothing shy of savage. "I'm sorry I didn't mention it earlier. The separation is new and I don't go around announcing my marriage status to every stranger."

Stranger? That stung but from the anger in his gaze, that's what he'd intended. She shook her head, sad that he couldn't just be straight with her. "You've been separated for three years. Muriel doesn't even live on the same side of town as you. Reese told me over the phone last night. How can you look me in the eyes and tell me this separation is new?"

Running his hands roughly through his hair, he turned and slammed the door. "You want to do this now?"

"Why not? Because last time you were in my room with me, you touched me like you used to and I tore myself up thinking you were a married man. And you aren't! You just like to pretend you are so things stay confusing."

"I don't have to explain myself to you, Samantha. I did that shit for years with Muriel, and that's the one good thing that came out of being single. I don't have to answer to anyone. Especially not some spoiled…" He waved his hand, and scrunched up his face.

"By all means," she gritted out. "Continue." *Being a dick.*

"Mouthy, nosy…woman!"

He threw the last word out like it was just as awful as the rest. Oh, she could see it now. Muriel had jaded him good. It wasn't that Bron wasn't right for her right now. He wasn't right for any woman. Not until he got over whatever Muriel had done to him.

"Spoiled," she said, pointing her index finger up in the air. "I lived in this tiny house, with a father who was a murderin' sonofabitch. I was shunned by the entire town, and my one solace was that you still pretended to love me. And you left me for someone you didn't give two shits about, so let's just put it all out there. I meant so little to you, that you chose someone you had no feelings for over me. I moved away from everything I knew and loved to find out Momma was sick and couldn't work anymore. And Dad wasn't exactly bringing home the bacon from prison. I worked three jobs to support us and pay for Momma's care, and most days it was hard to put food on the table. I took care of her. I watched her fade away, alone. And after I got her hospital bills all paid up, I worked my way from an assistant to a decent job that pays for my ratty one room apartment and the mortgage and bills on this place. Don't you ever call me spoiled again, Bronson Grady Cress. You don't know me. Not anymore. Your choice." Damn the tremor in her voice.

His look had softened with every sentence until his gaze dropped to her small suitcase in the corner. "I was pissed off at the situation we're in, and I shouldn't have taken it out on you. I'm sorry. I didn't know it was like that when you left here."

"Well, that was just fine by me. I didn't want you knowing my struggle. Not after what you did."

"I don't want to talk about Muriel anymore with you."

"Fine," she said tiredly. "Talking to you doesn't get me anywhere anyway. Sorry it didn't work out with you two." Not for Muriel, she could jump off a cliff without floaties, but for Bron. It was pretty plain and obvious he'd been through the ringer with his ex. And as angry and confused as he left Samantha, the thought of him being hurt curdled her stomach.

"I hate fighting with you," he said low, his eyes cast down to the metal legs of the bed.

"You always did."

"We were never any good at it." A smirk took his lips. It wasn't a smile yet, but she'd take it. "I think we only fought every once in a while so we could make up."

Memories of his kisses, his careful petting to reassure her he still cared and that he always would, no matter what, burned through her. She looked away. "Don't do that."

"Do what?"

"Don't take a trip down memory lane when everything is so messed up. Thinking about how it used to be—how *we* used to be—hurts me."

"Did you think about me when you left?"

Pain slashed through her chest and she wanted to deny it. To punish him for the choices he'd made. But what good would that do them now? "Of course I did." Her voice came out a ragged whisper. "You were all I wanted back then. But what good did thinking about you do for me?" Tears burned her eyes and she blinked them away. "You didn't feel the same, and you weren't pining for me back here."

His gaze looked agonized, tortured, and seeing him in so much pain made it hard to breathe. He turned and opened the door, but hesitated at the edge of the hallway. "You're wrong."

The click of the closing door echoed such a lonely sound.

****

If she left now, she'd have to come up with the extra three thousand dollars for Bron and his crew to do the detail work. She couldn't pay that outright on top of the main bill, so she'd have to put it on credit card.

Problem one was she hated owing anyone money after paying all those hospital bills.

Problem two was her one card she used to build credit didn't have a high line, and she would have to up the limit to cover that kind of money.

Problem three came when she called said credit card company, and they raised her credit line a measly five hundred dollars and told her to try for more in thirty days.

Damn, damn, double damn, and she was stuck staring at the tattoo that kept peeking out from under Bron's sleeve as he worked.

Her hormones were trying to kill her.

And it wasn't like she was attracted to a complete stranger. She was attracted to a stranger with carnal, intimate knowledge of her. And oh, she remembered how he was in bed. She hadn't been able to stop remembering. She'd touched herself countless times to his memories over the years, which had only seared her desire for him in her mind even more securely.

And he was good at touching her. If he'd been that accommodating to her needs when they were teenagers, how good must Bron-the-Man be in the bedroom now?

"You're staring again," Dillon observed. He was standing above her on a wobbly ladder, scraping the old popcorn texture off the ceiling. The corners of his vibrant blue eyes crinkled with his obnoxious smile.

"Was not," she muttered, and turned her back on them both. Sure, Bron could hang sheetrock like he was born to do it, with his sexy arms flexing every time he moved...

She snuck one last glance at Bron before ripping off another long strip of blue painter's tape. He was measuring for a cut with a box knife, and had a pencil clenched in his sexy mouth. He turned his head toward her like he could hear her thoughts, and embarrassed, she flinched away.

Smooth. And Pathetic.

The man had chosen someone else and here she was, a grown woman still pining for him. She was as crazy as her old man.

After she finished taping up the edges of the living room, she made the boys sandwiches from the groceries she'd bought in town yesterday and escaped to her room with her own lunch. She'd checked her email at the cafe yesterday too, like the busy responsible little bee she was. And though the Wi-Fi was sketchy, she was able to download the script her boss, Barbara, had sent her.

The deadline was tight, but it always was, so she wasn't stressed. If she could record her lines now, she'd be able to email the file back to Barbara tonight. This was the only way she had convinced her manager to let her to take an indefinite leave of absence from work when she'd found out Trent passed away. And since the one-A town of Joseph didn't boast a studio of any kind, Samantha had brought the equipment she needed with her.

115

Her voice sounded best in the closet, so she plugged in her laptop, closed the door and watched the twenty-five minute silent cartoon as she ate her sandwich and chips. This episode was about the main character, Riley, trying to solve the mystery of the missing vowels. Very educational.

Taking a big swig of cool water, she pressed record and dipped her voice to the softer tone she adopted when she was voicing Riley. Thirty minutes of getting every line recorded just right, and she zipped the file and prepared it to email Barbara as soon as she got in the cafe's Wi-Fi range again.

Kicking open the door from her cramped position, she almost screamed when she saw Bron stretched out on her bed.

"What are you doing in here?"

"Listening to you talk like a little girl. Is that some kinky thing you do for Ryan Cummings?"

"No! It's my job." And the way he always said Ryan's last name was annoying. Like Bron didn't really believe he existed or something. "And furthermore, why would you think we get our jollies off reciting lines about a little girl and her vowels?"

"I don't know. That's what I was waiting to ask

you."

"Who's nosy now?" she grumbled, heaving herself from the tiny closet. Kicking the laptop cord out of the way, she noticed the drawer to her desk slightly open. She ran her fingers over the opening, and the glossy sheen of the top photograph shone through the darkness.

"Why did you leave those here?" Bron asked. "I understand the refrigerator and your dad's old records. But why that stack of pictures?"

Her hand shook with her anger, and she clenched it against her side as she turned slowly. "I don't want you touching my things. They're mine, and you have no right."

He stood and clenched his own hands. "Those pictures are of me, too. And Trent." His voice cracked on his brother's name.

She felt like the grit on the floorboards beneath her feet. Without a word, she rifled through the pictures and took out several. Trent was grinning so big in every one of them. She kept two back and handed him the rest. "I'm sorry. I've been trying to not think about what happened to him. Sometimes it's nice to pretend he's not gone. I forget how hard

117

this must be on you."

Bron swallowed hard and took the pictures from her outstretched hand. His fingers brushed her knuckle and she stifled a gasp at the trill feeling his skin against hers caused. He shuffled through the pictures slowly and pressed his thumb against the last one.

"I left them here because I was hurt and I wanted to let you go," she explained, hoping it would ease the suffocating tension hanging in the air between them. "I wanted to let all of you go and not think about this place anymore. I knew wherever I was going, I wouldn't find what I had here."

Thickly, he said, "We're ahead of schedule and the boys will work until dark. I have another job to see about. I'll be here again tomorrow." He still hadn't taken his eyes from the last picture, one of all four of them by the creek, arms slung across each other's shoulders and laughing about something.

Bron escaped the room, and the front door shut a little too firmly as he left the house. Outside, his truck engine roared and he spun out on the gravel as he drove away.

She watched his truck disappear through her

bedroom window. He was so confounding. If he didn't like her answers, why did he insist on asking her the hard questions?

She looked down at the two pictures in her hands. One was of them all gathered around the dinner table at Bron and Trent's house. Mr. Cress must've taken this picture. It was a candid shot of them all talking, and Trent was the only one looking at the camera. He'd grown out his dark hair that year and it almost looked shaggy. Reese had loved it long like that, but he only kept it like that through sophomore year. Samantha had always loved this picture of all of them.

She'd kept the other one back because it was the only one she had of just her and Trent. He was giving her a knuckle sandwich and making a goofy face at the camera.

Grabbing her wallet and tossing the pictures onto the bed, she made for the front door.

"Where are you going?" Dillon asked.

"Town."

"Good. You should probably go look at paint colors while you're there. Tell me what you pick out tomorrow and I'll order what we need."

"Sure. Thanks, boys," she said as she left.

The paint store could wait, because right now, all she could think about was laying fresh flowers on Trent's grave and saying goodbye like she hadn't been able to do in front of the crowd at his funeral. She hadn't wanted to just throw dirt on his casket and go. She'd wanted to talk to him. Apologize for losing contact. He'd been important to her childhood, and he'd died not knowing how much she appreciated him.

If she could change it all, she would.

The grocery store was busy, and she had to wait in line for a while with the bouquet of gerbera daisies. She didn't know what the appropriate cemetery flower was, but she picked out orange ones, Trent's favorite color when they were kids.

The cemetery overlooked the old middle school and she parked right where she had a couple of days ago. Her throat was already raw by the time she walked up the pebbled path toward his grave marker. She froze when she saw Bron standing over his brother's grave. She couldn't hear anything from this far, but his jaw moved like he was talking.

She shouldn't interrupt his time here, so she began to back away. But just as she turned to go,

Bron reached under his sunglasses and rubbed his eyes and she couldn't just stand here and let him shoulder such sadness alone.

He was going to filet her when she approached, but she was growing used to it by now. Even if it hurt, it would be worth it to try.

Cradling the flowers, she weaved through the headstones until she stood just behind him. Bron wasn't talking anymore and his shoulders had gone stiff.

"Bron?" she said, in a tiny, trembling voice.

His tensed shoulders lifted with his breath and she thought he would just ignore her. Instead, he spun and crushed her to him. Burying his face against her neck, he squeezed her so tightly, she couldn't breathe. But he was breaking open right in front of her, and she couldn't find it in herself to complain about discomfort at a time like this.

"I found him," he said, voice raw. "I smelled the fire and knew something was wrong. I sped to the mill but it was too late and I couldn't get inside fast enough. I found him but he was already gone. I fought with him right before. A half an hour before he died, I was telling him to get his shit together."

"Shhh," she cooed, as hot tears slipped to her cheeks. "He knew you loved him."

"I've hurt everyone I've ever known," he said, gently pushing her away.

Without another word, he left her there, clutching her crumpled flowers and weeping over how hard it would be for a man like Bron to ever forgive himself.

He was the type to hold onto old guilt. He carried so much burden, more than she probably even realized. And all of his secrets and loss would pile up until it was a tower. And being the king of that tower would come with a price.

And that price could be his ability to find happiness.

SEVEN

Bron didn't show up the next day like he said he would, but Samantha wasn't surprised, or even curious about his absence. On the contrary, she was relieved. Their moments together at the cemetery had been heavy. Much heavier than she'd ever thought they would have again, and if she was perfectly honest, the intensity of her feelings scared her.

Time away from him felt necessary.

Instead, he sent another worker, Grant, who seemed to fit right in with the crew and who was very quiet. Dillon was comfortable and joked around with her a lot, but the other two seemed to steer clear while she painted the walls in the colors Dillon had picked up earlier. And when all three of the men climbed the ladder outside to repair the roof, she was able to blare the music and paint as she pleased.

Reese had done a bang-up job of avoiding all three of her phone calls. Whatever had happened with Dodger's cult that night had scared Reese away from her. Hopefully she was okay.

The only person who seemed completely unaffected by whatever mystery destruction she'd brought to Joseph was Dillon, who was singing an Aerosmith song at the top of his lungs for all the neighbors to hear. He had a decent voice too, so she bobbed her head and rolled paint, and hummed along with him much too low for any of them to hear. Her singing voice wasn't as awesome, and could be compared to a rabid opossum trying to hit high notes.

Humming, though—humming she could do.

A shadow covered the window and she turned. Bron walked up to the porch, then turned away and disappeared. The murmur of the men's voices could be heard from outside, but Bron sounded frustrated, and in a few moments, he was back at the door, staring at it intensely like it required an unknown password.

She lowered her paint roller and watched him turn again and leave. What the hell was he doing?

A clipped out, "Fuck," echoed down the street, and Bron threw the door open. "I brought this for you."

In his hand dangled a heavy looking paper bag that smelled suspiciously like key lime pie from the diner. It used to be her favorite.

"For yesterday. I needed to…thank you. And apologize. I should've kept it together better."

"Don't apologize for that," she whispered. Him letting her hold him at the cemetery had been the most real moment she could remember ever sharing with him. If he took it back, it would cut her deeply.

He didn't seem to want to come any closer than the entryway, so she tried for small talk. "Did you sleep any better last night?"

"No. Slept in the truck again."

"Why are you doing that? Sleep in your own bed. I know you own one. I saw two in your cabin."

He frowned and looked out the front window at the street out front.

"Wait," she mused. "Have you been sleeping in front of my house? No. Sorry, that sounded crazy."

His tongue slipped out to moisten his lips and his chest rose as he inhaled deeply. "Don't be mad."

"Are you sleeping outside my house?"

"Just until things settle down."

"Am I really in that much danger?"

"I told them you were mine, so it's my responsibility—"

"I'm not your responsibility, Bron. I'm a big girl now. If I'm in trouble, I need to know what to look for so I can watch out for myself."

"So, you don't want the pie?"

"Of course I want the pie. I swear if you tease me with it, then take it away, I'll paint your face Carriage House green," she said, reading off the paint can. "And I know you're changing the subject."

He set the bag on the dining table and winced at her paint job. "Have you ever done this before?"

"Painted a house?" she asked. "Never."

He stared at the scribble scrabble lines she'd made with the roller and frowned.

His disgruntled look made her feel defensive. She would fix it eventually. "But, you know…how hard can it be?"

"Geez, okay, well first off, you don't draw

pictures."

"I didn't!"

"There's a giant smiley face."

She giggled when she saw it. "Okay, so I drew one picture on accident." She sighed. "Fine. Teach me your ways."

"Give me that," he said, reaching for the roller. "This is too much paint on here, and when you get it to this consistency, you do long, steady strokes."

The way he said the word *strokes* drew her focus to his lips. He hadn't shaved this morning, and stubble graced his masculine jaw. Her fingers itched to reach out and touch it, just to see how it felt.

"Samantha?"

"Mmm hmm, long strokes."

"Samantha," he repeated in a low, annoyed tone. "I didn't come in here to do the work for you. I have another job site I'm managing. Learn, woman."

"Fine," she said, keeping her pout inside. She'd been relieved when he hadn't showed up this morning, but now that he was actually being civil, she didn't want him to leave. Fickle heart.

"Like this," he murmured, stepping behind her and wrapping his hand around hers. Moving the roller up slow and steady, he paused and brought it back down.

Pulse tripping, breath hitching, body heating, knees quaking, she tried to keep it together as he brushed his fingers to her wrist and held her gently as she moved to paint more of the wall.

She stifled a gasp as his other hand slid onto her hip bone as he guided her farther down the wall. A burning warmth started in her chest and spread downward, pooling just above her thighs. If she didn't breathe soon, she was going to pass out.

He moved his hand from her wrist to her shoulder and she could feel the heat from his chest against her back. He dropped his chin, and the delicious rasp of his stubble brushed her oversensitive cheek. When his chest finally touched her back, she could feel his thrumming heartbeat through the thin material of their shirts, and she sighed heavily and leaned back to soak in his warmth. God, she'd missed him.

"Is Ryan real?" he asked in a soft stroke against her ear.

"Yes."

"Are you his?"

"I was on a blind date with him when Reese called. He's a weasel-faced ninny-pecker."

Bron huffed a laugh and pulled the roller from her hand, dropped it into the paint pan, then turned her slowly. "So, you lied about what he was to you—"

"Misled you."

"You mislead me about your relationship with the man, and then you fileted me for withholding the status of my separation and divorce. Is that the right of it?"

"Well, when you put it like that..." All sexy, with that pouty lip she wanted to bite, she did feel a little bad for her reaction.

Running his hands down her arms, he gripped her wrists, brought them above her head, and pressed her against the wall. The new paint was in serious jeopardy of butt smudges, but fuck it all. Bron's eyes were burning into hers like he was incapable of looking away, and she had to make a conscious effort not to melt into a puddle and slide through the scratched up floorboards.

"No more stripping me down, woman. I'm not the same as I was, and you're going to have to forgive and forget, or our friendship doesn't work."

He pressed his hips against hers, and despite his steely grip on her arms and invasion of her personal space, she didn't feel trapped at all. She felt hungry for more. Even as she burrowed against him, it wasn't enough. Tipping his chin, he lowered his lips to hers. The most embarrassing helpless sound wrenched from her throat as his jaw worked, and he nudged his tongue past her lips. She would remember to be mortified when the sound didn't cause Bron to push his impressive erection harder against her belly.

If this is what he called friendship, Bron was officially the greatest friend of all time. They should make a friend hall of fame, and just line the hallways with pictures of his sexy face.

His tongue lapped hers and she clenched her hands against the urge to fight his grip and touch the skin just under the hem of his T-shirt.

"Hey, boss?" Dillon asked from the porch. "Oh, shit, this is happening."

Bron pulled away by an inch and turned his head. "Get out."

"Yep, on my way." Dillon still stood there, watching and rocking his weight from heels to toes and back again.

A muscle twitched beneath Bron's left eye. "What, Dillon?"

"Congratulations."

"Get. The fuck out," Bron growled.

Samantha pursed her lips to stifle the laugh bubbling up from her throat.

Bron looked pissed, and she dropped her forehead to his chest and let out a happy sigh.

"I Googled Ryan Cummings," he muttered. "He looks like a tool."

"Gasp! You stalked my fake boyfriend? Careful, Bronson. That's getting dangerously close to more-than-friendship territory."

A chuckle rattled from him, and she pressed her cheek against his chest so she could feel the vibrations from that consuming sound.

"At the cemetery earlier, that was the first time I've been able to lean on anyone," he said against the top of her hair, serious once again. "It's not usually my thing, but it was nice not feeling alone for a moment."

"It used to be me and you against the world."

"Things are different now though," he whispered, wrapping his arms around her waist and pulling her closer. "You have to know that. Feel it."

"What are you saying?" Why did it always feel like he was building up to hurt her again?

"I'm saying I think we should do lunch at the cafe, like you and Reese did. I think we should try to be friends again, because all this despising each other shit has my head messed up. I hate it. With all the stuff that's going on behind the scenes in my life, I need something more steady right now. And if you're here for a week, I can't go a full seven days not knowing if you're going to roast me every time you see me."

She loved hearing his voice while feeling the rumble of it against her face. Easing away, she leaned her shoulder blades back against the wall and offered her hand for a shake. "A casual, middle-of-the-day lunch between friends."

Leaning forward, he playfully nipped at her bottom lip with his teeth and shook her hand, then turned it over and brushed his lips against her knuckles. "I'll pick you up tomorrow. Wear pants."

"Har, har," she said sarcastically as he walked out the front door. She'd been sure to wear her pajama pants when she opened up the door this morning, but he'd missed the effort on account of playing hooky.

Tomorrow she would wear a skirt just to let him know she couldn't be bossed around.

****

What was he doing? Bron was in way over his head and had been getting there steadily ever since Sam blew into town. And now he was conjuring all these protective instincts from his bear that would do nothing but get them both hurt, or worse.

Dodger was going to maul him.

The alpha's house sat right off of East First. It was a historic Victorian style home he shared with his mate.

Bron was stalling going into the war zone.

What was he supposed to do though? When she'd been caught at the meeting, the other shifters had bloodlust written all over their faces. He couldn't just stand by while they hurt a human. No. She was more than that. She was his human, she just didn't know to the extent he was willing to go to protect her yet.

Yet? Like he was going to tell her he turned into a monster a couple times a week. She'd run, and this time, she wouldn't come back. He hadn't wished he was human even once in the last six years, but she had him questioning everything. And for the life of him, he couldn't figure out if that was a good thing or bad.

He had to stop being a pussy and just do this. Pumping his hands a couple of times to ramp his bear up, he walked up the stone pathway and knocked on Dodger's door.

The old biker didn't greet him with a smile and a clap on the back like he normally did, only opened the door and jerked his head in silent invitation.

Inside the pristine and sparsely decorated home, Bron sat at the dining room table and bounced his knee nervously as the alpha took the seat across from him.

"Boy, what have you done?" Dodger asked.

"Nothing." Yet. "I haven't claimed her and she's only here for a week. I'm fixing up her house as fast as possible and then she's gone. Sam won't be any trouble for us. I promise."

"Sounds like the promises of a man who cares too much. Have you forgotten whose blood runs through her veins? Or are you just so lovesick you've forgotten."

"You don't know what we went through when we

were younger. We were bonded. It's hard to break it."

Dodger slammed his fists on the table. "Don't talk to me about how hard it is to break some bullshit bond, Cress. You do it for your people. We all make sacrifices, and this one's on you. Are you really willing to go through banishment for her?"

"Give me a week. Let me finish her house. Hell, I'll buy the damned thing off her if it'll make her leave faster."

"And what's your motivation?"

Bron rubbed his hands over his eyes like it would relieve the headache building there. "I don't want her hurt."

"I need to know where your head's at, because when it comes down to her leaving, I need to know you can let her go."

Bron scrubbed his hands over his face until his stubble made a scratching sound against the palms of his hands. "I can let her go. I did it before, and I'll do it again."

Dodger raised his eyebrows and canted his head like he didn't believe a word Bron said. "She's human, and you're the last of the Cress line. None of the bears left can afford to take a mate who is a genetic dead-end. We're seventy-five left in the world and we just lost Trent. We're about as endangered as you can get, and you're *this* close to your alpha term. Don't fuck this up over a woman. And don't put us in the path of those Hunters again. For all we know she's the reason Trent was killed too. She's poison to our kind." The chair creaked as the lanky alpha leaned back and crossed his arms. "You have one week to get her out of town. If she's still here when that time is up, I'll take matters into my own hands, and I ain't afraid to get 'em bloody, you savvy?"

Oh, Bron savvied all right. Getting to alpha rank was a bloody process, and not for the weak at heart. It's why Dad never made it that far, and why Trent never tried. Cress blood in the alpha rank was important for tradition, and it was up to Bron and the bloodthirsty grizzly that lived inside of him to succeed.

He was second right now, but only because he'd fought just about every dominant bear to get here. And if he could hold this spot when Dodger's ten year term was up next month, the position of alpha would fall to him. Did he want the responsibility of the entire clan of remaining bear shifters' survival on his shoulders? Not particularly. But his bear was made to lead. It was in Bron's lineage and he'd worked hard to get where he was, just like his ornery cuss of a father had trained him to do.

"I understand, and I have no intention of being banished. She'll be gone in a week." Bron stood to leave.

"One last thing," Dodger drawled. "I got a call from Marsden this morning. He says you've been ignoring Muriel's calls."

"So?"

"So, if there's a chance at reconciliation with her, you'll do it and keep our clans allied. There's too few of us left to be bickering and murdering each other off."

Bron shook his head slowly. "I'm not doing that again. I've given enough to try and make that alliance work."

"It wasn't a fucking suggestion, boy. I'm your alpha still and that's an order. Pick up your damned phone when she calls."

Red fury seared up Bron's spine and his bear roared to be let loose inside him. Leaning against the table, he leveled Dodger a look and gritted out, "Don't you call me *boy* again or I'll lay you out, alpha or no. You said I can't have Samantha because she's human. Fine. I get that. But I ripped myself to shreds trying to make a pairing work with Muriel, and I'm not stupid enough to try for another round. I'll choose who I take to my bed from here on. Find another bear to breed her."

"You're walking a dangerous line disobeying me like this."

"Save your threats. You gave me a week with Samantha. Muriel is off the table. I'm not playing puppet dick to this clan's whims anymore."

He slammed the door on his way out and wanted to yell his anger until his roar sent all the roosting birds to flight in the trees around him. His insides were being shredded from the animal trying to claw his way out of him, and if he didn't find some woods and soon, he was going to change right here on the main drag for all the unassuming humans in town to see.

Fighting to stay human, he jumped in his Ford and sped through town. He needed to be watching Samantha's house tonight, because no matter what Dodger said about giving him a week, that alpha wasn't trustworthy. Never had been, never would be. It was part of what made him so good at his job.

Clan first, fuck everyone else.

Bron's bear was coming, and he wasn't going to make it to the cabin. Jerking the truck off the road, he stumbled from the cab and pulled at his shirt and jeans, and ran as far as he could manage into the tree line.

His spine cracked in a hundred little machine gun bursts, and he pitched forward onto his hands and knees. His snarl of pain turned to a roar as his beast slowly shredded him. Bones stretching and face elongating, he gasped at the blinding pain right before the prickle of fur burst from his skin. He stood on two legs and raised his nose to the coming night. He bellowed a promise that if Dodger or any of his clan touched a hair on Samantha's head, he'd maul every last one of them.

She'd eased his pain over Trent's death with nothing more than an embrace and soft words.

She made him feel again.

Her life was his to protect.

EIGHT

Two rooms were now painted and it was useless trying to get any of the dried drops of Wisp of Mauve out of her hair. Bron wouldn't care, but she wanted to look nice for him. Even if it was just a casual meal between friends, he'd let her know he still had feelings for her with his affection yesterday.

Hope bloomed in her like the opening morning glories creeping up the south wall of the house.

She fussed with her dark tresses, picking and plucking until at least the front was free of splattered paint. Dillon catcalled from the front room, which could only mean one thing.

Bron was here.

Nervous flutters bumped around her belly as she

smoothed her black A-line skirt. It hit above her knees, and though the breeze outside was laced with the chill of autumn, she made up for the show of skin by pairing it with knee-high boots and a warm purple sweater.

Bron was in the middle of play-punching Dillon in the stomach, and his smile was easy as he talked too low for her to hear. A subtle crook of his too masculine lips and a flash of white teeth, and she was mesmerized by his smile. When she moved toward him, his gaze collided with hers and his mouth dipped open for a moment. A slow rake of his eyes down her figure and back was enough to turn those butterflies in her stomach to dragons.

"Damn, Samantha," Dillon said. "You clean up nice."

"You're fired," Bron muttered as he offered a hand to her. "You ready?"

"You aren't really firing him, are you?"

"You don't have to champion me, Sam," Dillon said with a solemn shake of his head. The blue in his eyes was practically dancing. "If Bronson doesn't fire me three times by Tuesday, it's a slow week."

She laughed and slipped the palm of her hand

into Bron's.

"We'll be back in an hour," he said to his crew. "I want that ceiling textured when I get back or I really will consider firing your ass. Our timeline just jumped forward by two days."

Dillon's eyes narrowed. "You talked to Dodger?"

"He's given us a week. She needs to be gone in four days for me to feel good about this."

Dillon made a single clicking sound behind his teeth and twitched his head. "You got it, boss."

Four days? That seemed so soon. And permanent. And why was she being run out of town by his asshole cult leader anyway? What had she done? Not a damned thing, that's what, because being in the same genetic pool as her murderin' daddy wasn't a crime. And even if it were, she'd been punished enough.

She opened her mouth to ask for details, but Bron turned and led her out to his truck. He buckled her in like he'd done the night of the meeting, and looked distracted as he hopped behind the wheel.

"Are you going to explain why I have to be out of town in four days?"

"Nope."

"I checked for your truck last night out in front of my house."

"I had somewhere I had to be."

"Good," she said triumphantly. "So you're starting to trust me to take care of myself?"

The engine roared and gears clicked into place. "I trust you to take care of yourself in normal circumstances. This is different though. Look, I can't tell you everything you want to know."

"Because you're in a cult. Which I don't understand, because you don't seem the type." She watched his knuckles turn white as he gripped the steering wheel. "I'm worried about you."

"Well, lady, if you really knew me, you wouldn't spare me that worry. I'm fine. And I'm not in a cult, so stop calling it that."

Two steps forward, one step back with just a few sentences that proved how quickly he could shut her out and distance himself.

A short, irritated growl sounded from his throat. "I can't talk about this stuff, and it's not just because Dodger told me not to. It's to keep you safe. Can you just trust me on this and let things go? If I tell you to drop something, it's for your own good."

"And yours, so you don't actually have to conduct a deep conversation with me. Which would be fine if we were strangers, but contrary to whatever you think about me not really knowing you, we aren't. Our history is way too long and wide to be pretending like that. So, keep your secrets and keep me an arm's length away, and see if I stick around for that shit, Bronson."

"There is no benefit in this for me but to spend time with you."

"What does that mean?"

He pulled onto East First and parked the truck at the end of the cracked pavement. Turning his smoldering gaze to her, he said, "You have the power to hurt me in more ways than you even know. This is a risk for me, and I can see it in your eyes, you don't like the way I have conversations and avoid your questions. I'm telling you right now, you don't want to open that can of worms, darlin'. You want to help me get this house done, leave when you're supposed to, and forget about me and everyone else in this fucked up town. You have to move on with your life."

"Then why are we here? Why did you invite me out to lunch? Is it to mess with my head? Make me care about you again so it takes another six years to try and date anyone? God, Bron, I'm so tired of fighting with you. It's not my personality to be confrontational, and it's draining me. But you give me nothing." She wrapped her arms around her chest like a shield. "You're going to break me again."

His voice came out so soft, she had to strain to hear. "How can I break you? You don't even know me anymore."

"Bullshit. You keep telling yourself that to push me away because you're afraid of whatever is happening between us. I know your heart. Even if you aren't the same boy I used to know, I can still see the good in you."

He shook his head and donned a humorless smile as he tracked two elderly ladies making their way up the sidewalk in front of the truck. His wrist was draped over the steering wheel, but he looked anything but relaxed. Even his fist was clenched.

"I wonder if you knew what I was, would you still care about me?" he said, sliding a challenging gaze to her.

"If you don't tell me what is happening to you, you'll never know if I'm strong enough to accept everything. What are you?" A cult member? She got that, and she was already hatching plans to get him out of Dodger's grasp. He didn't need those manipulative people for emotional support, or whatever it was they provided him with. She was going to find him help.

"I'm an animal."

His admission drew her up short. It shocked and saddened her that he could see himself like that. "My dad is a murderer. I've seen men who were animals, Bron. You're not one." She leaned across his seat and brushed her lips against the smooth planes of his cheek and let them linger. He smelled of shaving cream and Bron, and something richer, deeper...something new. She inhaled and pressed his scent to memory, just another thing about him that had changed.

She trailed her lips to his neck and tasted his skin—heady and masculine. Little by little, his fist unclenched over the steering wheel.

"What are you doing to me, woman?" he asked in a husky voice.

"Caring for you, just as I always have."

He pulled her into his lap and checked the elderly

ladies' progress down the road. "I wish I could tell you everything," he murmured, brushing his fingertips up the back of her knee. "Show you everything about me and see if you'd still feel the same. It's just not a risk I can take."

"Ever?"

Splaying his fingers, he ran his hand up her skirt against the inside of her thigh. "I punished you the other day, and brought you to the edge. And then I listened to you cry in your room because of the pain I'd caused you."

Her breath hitched as fire spread through her at his languid touch. He hadn't answered her question, but right now, she was having trouble caring about anything other than his slow ascent up her skirt.

"Do you think about me when you touch yourself?" he whispered, watching her mouth.

Her voice came out low and breathy. "Yes."

His fingers reached the frilly panties she'd worn for him, and her knees spread apart without her telling them to. Easing the lingerie down her legs and over her boots, he tossed them onto the empty seat and cradled the back of her head, easing her mouth to his.

147

The kiss was slow, and burning. He drew her bottom lip into his mouth and sucked gently until her insides were rolling with desire. It was so easy to imagine his tongue lapping other places on her body, and a deep shiver took her body.

"Mmm," he moaned. "I remember you used to do that when I found a new place you liked me to touch you."

He gripped the inside of her thigh, massaging rhythmically, teasing her.

Wriggling in desperation to be closer, she whimpered as his knuckle skimmed her sex.

"I want to know what you taste like," he whispered against her neck. He ran his finger up her seam, spreading the wetness he'd conjured there, separating her slick folds until her legs shook.

If he left her wanting this time, she'd explode.

The rattle of a zipper sounded, and wide-eyed, she looked down in time to see him free his cock from the confines of his jeans. Red, hard and bulging, he gripped the base and pulled up long and slow. He was thicker than she remembered and her breaths came in pants as he slid his finger inside her.

Geez, what was she doing? She was fooling

around in Bron's truck in broad daylight like they were a couple of rutting teenagers. Thank the powers that be that the town seemed to be utterly dead on a Tuesday afternoon. And for dark window tint.

She couldn't take her eyes off the bead of moisture that pushed from the tiny seam of his cock. She wanted to taste it—wanted to taste all of him.

The rhythm of his slowly pumping fist matched the pace he set with his finger inside of her. Withdrawing all the way, he slowly pushed into her again as he ran his hand down the length of him.

"I want to watch you come," she whispered. This was the sexiest thing she'd ever seen.

Angling his elbow, he pushed into her slick sex to the knuckle and spread his knees wider. A groan came from his throat as he pulled a long, hard stroke against himself. "Only if you come with me," he said, grazing his teeth against the fabric of her sweater.

Arm thrown around his neck, skirt clenched up in her free hand, she nodded jerkily. She was going to detonate soon, and every brush of his hand against her clit brought her that much closer. Every muscle built with pressure, and a tiny part of her wanted to beg him to ram her hard and deep. He was taking it slow though, and the pleasure was too consuming to find anything wrong with the punishingly gradual pace he was setting.

His hips moved and the muscles in his arms tensed. His eyes rolled back in his head, and he leaned his forehead against her arm like he was losing control of himself. His shaft, growing thicker as he fisted it, brushed her side, and she lifted the hem of her shirt so she could feel the moisture at the tip.

Her breath shook as he pulled his thumb over the head of his cock and stroked up and down. His movements became jerkier and he pressed his finger into her harder and faster. He was close and she was right there, teetering on the edge. Closing his eyes and gritting his teeth, he ground out, "Sam," as the first hot shot hit her skin.

She pressed his shirt up to watch streams of milky white spray the pale skin over his taut stomach as she exploded around his finger. Orgasm crashed through her, clamping around him as he threw his head back and released one last surge of cum.

His hooded eyes looked lighter than they had minutes earlier, but he closed them and hunched into himself with one final aftershock as she pulsed around his hand. When he opened them again, they looked normal. She didn't remember how much his eye color shifted from before, but maybe it was just like that with people who had such strange, bright hues to begin with.

She sagged against this chest, panting and spent. Which was confusing because she hadn't done a damned thing but watch Bron get them both off. It hadn't exactly been a vigorous workout, but here she was, feeling like she'd just run a mile on a treadmill and wondering if she could hook her panties with the heel of her boot so she didn't have to move the lazy half of her.

"You called me Sam," she whispered, trying not to ruin the magic of the moment. "I like that better than when you use my full name."

He grunted as he kissed her, pressing his tongue against hers in a slow pull. Sliding his finger from her, he pulled it to his mouth and sucked the length of it. Now it was his turn to shiver.

She should've been embarrassed, really she should have, but she'd wanted to taste him too, and watching him clean her off of his finger was almost as sexy as watching his jets of cum shoot up his six pack.

He brushed his wet fingertip against her full bottom lip, and she opened up and bit it gently, then sucked.

His eyes roiled with hunger as he watched her lips. "Woman, you're going to ruin me."

"Good," she breathed. Because she was pretty sure he'd already ruined her.

****

It was hard not to touch Bron after the intimacy they'd shared in his truck. He seemed to be suffering the same, because his hand never left the small of Samantha's back for long. And when they were seated in a booth in the cafe, he ran his hand up and down her arm until it was the warmest part of her body.

He donned a new shirt, courtesy of the five or so clean ones he kept in the back of his truck for work. It stretched tight over his chiseled torso and the broad width of his shoulders. And if she looked hard enough at the dark gray material, she could make out each abdominal swell in his hard stomach. Her cheeks turned hot every time she remembered him coming on himself. If she lived to be a thousand, she would never forget how turned on she'd been, watching his brows knit as he rasped her name and lost himself.

Food ordered and chocolate milkshakes settled in front of them, Bron rested his hand on the inside of her thigh and kissed her shoulder. "Sometimes I forget the last six years happened," he admitted. "When I look at you, it feels like no time has passed. All of the bad stuff just gets pushed behind."

Heat flushed her cheeks and she ducked her head shyly. "For me too. Being back here has been so hard, but then there are times when it feels like I never left at all. And then I look around and remember myself, and it leaves me feeling kind of breathless, you know?"

He smiled and dropped his gaze. "Yeah." Reaching into his pocket, he pulled out a rumpled movie ticket. "Look what I found a few years ago when I was cleaning out Muriel's belongings. I had a whole box of stuff from when we were kids in a closet that I'd forgotten about."

Plucking the tiny paper stub from his palm, she read the block lettering. *Ghostbusters*. "Oh my gosh," she breathed. "I remember this night. It was homecoming night junior year, and all four of us wanted to ditch the dance. And the drive-in was showing old movies that night."

"And Trent snuck in a flask of Dad's Maker's Mark."

"Yes! And we all got shit-faced because we'd never had anything to drink before. That was the night Reese sang opera through the end credits from the bed of your old Chevy, and got us kicked out before the double feature."

A grin stretched his face as he draped his arm around the back rest of her seat. "Do you remember after?"

"Of course I do." Heat flared up her neck. "Trent took Reese home, and you took me up to the old water tower. We climbed it and talked all night, overlooking the lights of the town."

"And?"

"When we came back down, that was the first time we were together, in the woods right under it."

He playfully nipped her ear, a delicious reward for her good memory, and leaned back so the waitress could set a pair of chicken fried steak dinners in front of them. How many times had they sat in this cafe and ordered just this?

A lifetime of memories stretched between them and she wondered how she was ever supposed to build something so intense with another man. "It'll be hard to leave on Saturday," she admitted quietly.

"But you have to. It's not safe for you here."

Somehow, she'd come back to find even more mysteries than when she'd left, and Bron seemed bound and determined not to enlighten her. It was hard to press him though when such sincerity pooled in the bright green depths of his eyes. He was worried for her. Whatever was threatening her here was real, even if she couldn't see it.

As scary as it was to do so, she trusted him.

"Someday, will you tell me why this is all happening? Will you tell me everything?"

He worried the corner of his lip with his teeth as he looked down at his steaming plate of food. "Best for you if I don't. You not knowing what is going on is the only reason you're still breathing."

Fear skittered up her spine at his chilling words. "Will you call me when I leave?" They hadn't spoken on the phone when she'd left last time, but this time around, it would rip her guts out to be severed from him completely again.

"How will either of us move on if I do?"

Her voice dipped to a whisper. "Won't you come

with me then? We could leave this place and start over, and no one would care if we were together."

His adam's apple dipped down and back up as he swallowed hard. "There are people I have to protect here. I couldn't run like that."

Couldn't or wouldn't? The difference mattered so much, she was too scared to ask. "What do we do then?"

The ghost of a smile brushed his lips. "We live like we mean it for the next four days. If this is all we get, we'll make it count."

She didn't want to point out that she was already falling in love with him again, and that every minute spent with him tethered her soul more tightly to his. He already seemed to feel it too, and what was the point of talking about the sad stuff they couldn't avoid? That would only waste their precious time together.

There would be no declarations of love or grand gestures. There would be no healing the past, because there simply wasn't enough time. They would have to fill every moment and make them count, and the memories here would have to last for the rest of her life. For the rest of his.

And for as unfair as she found it all, to have to leave him after finding him again, a peace settled over her that at least for a little while, she'd be with him.

And that was more than she thought she'd ever have again.

NINE

Bron had told Dillon they would be back in an hour, so naturally he gave them hell for showing up three hours later.

Did she regret the time with Bron? Absolutely not. They'd spent hours laughing and rehashing old memories and childhood stories. It felt so good to think about all of the happy times they'd had again. Forcing those memories from her mind had been a constant struggle over the past six years, and now, with the strain lifted, she realized just how tired it all made her. Now, she was practically swimming in a sea of relief.

Changed into her paint spattered work clothes again, she put her hair in a messy bun and popped the top of the paint can in the living room. Stirred and prepared, she poured it into her roller pan and stood, stretching her spine.

Her body hummed as Bron pressed behind her and kissed her neck. His teeth brushed her skin there, and he swatted her ass before heading outside to work on the porch with Grant and Dillon.

He was intoxicating like this. Talking about his brother at the diner, of all of the fun memories they had together, seemed to have eased something in him.

It made her wonder just how long he'd been dealing with everything alone. At least for the next four days, she could share the burden of what he'd been through.

As the day stretched on, the soundtrack of nail guns, saws and the low murmur men's voices as they worked together filled the evening air. Samantha worked hard and finished painting the last three rooms of the house. After all of the blue tape had been removed and tossed into a trash bag, she stood back and admired the open kitchen and living area. The new colors and lack of deteriorating wallpaper did wonders for the space. And even dirty and scuffed, the wood floors showed promise of being beautiful with some care.

She could be happy in a place like this.

"Sam," Bron called. "Come here. I want to show you something."

She scrubbed her hands together, dislodging the dried paint on her palms and stepped out onto the porch. Then she gasped.

Pressing her hand to her chest, she circled slowly to where Bron and the boys stood. The porch floorboards had been completely replaced, and new whitewashed columns held up the overhanging roof. But that wasn't the best part. The most surprising part of the complete transformation was the porch swing that swayed lazily in the breeze.

Her mouth was hanging open as she stared. She'd always wanted one, for as long as she could remember. "How did you know?"

Bron slid his arms around her shoulders and held her tight, then kissed her forehead and eased back like he couldn't help but watch her. "I remembered from before."

She must've told him at some point, but she couldn't recall an exact conversation about it.

Her eyes prickled with tears and she blinked them away. Stunned, she said, "I didn't think it was in the budget."

"It wasn't," Dillon piped up.

Bron twisted but she missed whatever look he gave his employee because she couldn't stop staring at the swing.

"This one's on me. I got it for a steal from the hardware store. It adds curb appeal."

He was fibbing. It wasn't just to add curb appeal and he knew it. He'd done it for her, because somewhere inside of him was the boy she remembered.

"You want to try it out?" he asked.

Dillon and Grant sauntered back inside and she sat gingerly on the swing.

"It won't fall. We replaced the beams up top for you, too."

The fool grin on her face couldn't be helped and she laughed as she rocked back. The rhythmic squeak of the metal chains sounded like home.

"I've missed that smile," he said softly.

He'd pulled his sunglasses back on, even though the day was chilly and overcast. She wished she could see his eyes when he said things like that.

"Sit by me?"

"Woman, I took a three hour lunch break and we're on a tight deadline."

"I'm your boss, right?"

His smile lines deepened. "I guess technically you're paying me for the work, so you could be considered my boss."

"I want you to sit by me, Bron, and then I want you to hold me tight and pretend that this could be us when we're old."

The smile dipped from his lips and he hesitated before striding over to her, boots making a hollow sound on the new wooden boards.

Settling beside her, he draped his arm around her shoulders and drew her into his side.

"Today has been perfect," she whispered as they watched the sun sink below the Seven Devils Mountains.

Drawing her legs into his lap, he hugged her closer. She couldn't see his face, because he was watching the sunset, but from here, his cheeks swelled like he was smiling. He'd done that a lot today.

He was so warm, she didn't even feel the chill of the oncoming night. His gray thermal shirt had the top button undone, and she could see the hard line bisecting his pecs that delved beneath the thin material.

He stood suddenly and walked into the house, and she thought she'd angered him somehow. But he came back moments later with a blanket and draped it around her shoulders, then kissed the top of her head and murmured, "I've got to get back to work. Why don't you take the night off? The walls look great."

She beamed under his compliment. They did look pretty good, if she did say so herself.

"I do need to run into town and check my work email. Maybe I'll get some more groceries to stock the fridge while I'm running around. You need anything?"

Ensnaring her with both hands on either side of her hips, he leaned forward and took a long pull of her lips. He angled his head and his tongue brushed her mouth, asking for an invitation in. Wrapping her arms around his neck, she gave into him, rolling her tongue against his as he sipped at her.

The blanket slipped from her shoulders as he

pressed her back, but she didn't care. She was greedy for his touch. With a love nip, she bit his bottom lip and a low rumble sounded from his chest. Before he could stop, she pressed her hand against his heartbeat to feel the vibration of the strange sound. It was something that had always been a part of him—a part of him that she loved.

"Why do you make that sound?" she asked.

"Because I want you," he said simply.

The sound was desire for him then, and she couldn't help the pride that swelled and filled her.

"Grrr," she said in a pathetic imitation.

He dropped his head against her chest and chuckled.

"Are you laughing at my love growl?"

"Yes," he croaked out. "It's cute. You're cute."

"Cute like a baby turtle, or cute like a sexy vixen who amuses you so much you want to ravage her every chance you get?"

He took her hand and pressed it against his erection in answer, then turned and sauntered away. "You're no baby turtle, Sam. You're pure trouble," he said with a devilish grin before he disappeared inside.

****

Samantha had intended for her trip to be a quick one, but she'd got sucked into skyping her boss and going over the rest of the week's deadline schedule, and it had taken half an hour to download the files she needed for work on account of the sketchy Wi-Fi that kept making her sign in over and over. She had to rush through grocery shopping because the store closed at eight, and by the time she got home, the crew, including Bron, had gone home for the day.

She tried to stifle the disappointment of missing him, but a note taped to the door made her bad timing a little easier to swallow.

Hey Trouble,
I need to take care of some stuff at home.
Be back soon.
-Bron

It was the same blocky, capital letter print writing she'd memorized from all of the notes he'd passed her in class when they were younger.

Folding it neatly, she opened the front door and pressed it into her desk drawer with the rest of the pictures from her past. After the groceries were unloaded, she cooked spaghetti and sautéed vegetables with a country station crooning to her about relaxing after a hard day's work. *Amen to that.*

Dishes cleaned, showered, legs shaved, face scrubbed and bed turned down, she recorded her lines for work in the closet and checked the window for the tenth time. This time, unlike the others, Bron's truck was parked across the street.

Flicking her fingertip away to lower the blind, she tried to steady her thundering heartbeat. She had a plan, but acting on it would make leaving on Saturday excruciating. But if she didn't, she'd never know how it was to be close to him again. She would always wonder, *what if?*

He'd said they needed to live like they meant it. But this? There would be no getting over ripping her heart open and letting him burrow inside.

Hang responsible decisions. She wanted him and the thought of denying herself his touch hurt too much. Sliding her feet into a pair of warm slippers, she wrapped a blanket around her shoulders and padded out onto the porch and down the sidewalk.

Bron opened the door to his pickup before she

even got there. "What's wrong?" he asked, frown marring his features.

Good grief, this was a really bad idea.

"If we only have four days left together, I don't want to spend any of that time apart."

"Okay. I had to take care of stuff at my house tonight though—"

"No, that's not what I'm saying." God, she was so awkward at this. She blamed it on zero adult experience at seducing a man. "I want you to stay with me. At nights. I mean I want you to sleep beside me."

The tension in his shoulders relaxed and he shut the door to his truck softly. "You want me to stay inside with you?"

"Yeah."

He dragged her waist to him and spun her until she was pressed against the side of his pickup. "And you just want me to sleep beside you? Because I'm telling you right now, you strip out of those ugly pajama pants in the middle of the night and brush those sexy little panties against me, and it won't be sleeping that's on my mind."

Oh, what that man did to her insides when he

talked like that.

"I bought condoms at the store." Hunching her shoulders, she squeezed her eyes closed in mortification at allowing him to see just how much planning she'd put into this. She opened one eye, but he didn't look surprised at all. In fact, he looked utterly satisfied and more than a little amused.

His gaze dipped to her lips and he pulled her flush against him. "Good."

Wrapping the blanket around him to keep them both warm, she stood on tiptoes and kissed him. Never in her lifetime could she ever tire of the feel of his mouth against hers, or the taste of him, and she only had four days to savor him completely.

His grip hardened around her waist, and with a nip at her neck, he folded her into his arms and carried her into the house. She expected ravaging and clothes ripping, but instead, he set her gently down in the bedroom and wrapped his arms around her, buried his face in her neck like he had at the cemetery.

"Are you sure about this?" he rasped against the oversensitive skin just under her ear.

Sure about it? Heck no. She was standing on the

edge of a cliff and the wrong step could cut them both down to nothing. But she was already too far in, so close to his ready body. She couldn't stop now if she tried.

"I'm sure I want to be with you. I always have."

As he eased back, she saw the agonized expression on his face just before his lips crashed onto hers. Head bobbing and jaws working, she was overwhelmed by his warm hands exploring her body. Shirt gone, and now her pants joined the growing pile on the floor.

Bron's hair was mussed in a sexy tostle from tugging his sweater off, and his smile was slow and thirsty as he stared at her breasts. They were full and swollen as her want turned to eagerness.

Leaning forward, he palmed her breasts, pushing one upward until it was angled toward him. Dipping his lips to her taut nipple, his tongue on her flesh brought a helpless moan from her as she gripped his hair.

Slow, languid licks, and she was beginning to think she could have an orgasm just from this. Her breath quickened as he moved his attention to the other side, and the slow rip of his zipper zinged a shiver of anticipation up her spine.

If he kept going, lapping at her as if she tasted like nectar, her knees were going to go out completely. As if he saw it coming, he pressed her back onto the edge of the bed and spread her knees wide.

Right. This was it. Reaching, she snatched a condom from the bedside table where she'd fanned them. He took it from her hand and tossed it to the floor. "Not yet, baby. We've got all night."

Oh. He pulled her panties down to her ankles in a slow seduction and bit the tender skin of her inner thigh. Oooh.

No, no, no, she wasn't comfortable with this. It was...she was...boys shouldn't kiss down there. "Wait—"

He rubbed his hands up the inside of her legs and squeezed until she could see his fingers indent in her soft flesh. "You changed your mind?" Concern flashed through his eyes, so light, she couldn't tell if they were green or blue anymore.

"No. Just...you don't have to do that."

His lip curled up on one side. "Woman, I'm not doing it because I have to. I'm doing it because I want to taste you. Your smell has been driving me mad for days. I want more."

"It's not weird for you?"

A deep chuckle reverberated in his throat and he looked her dead in the eye when he said, "Not at all."

"Okay." She had tensed her legs in protest, but relaxed again as he massaged her calf and pressed a kiss against her ankle, then trailed his lips to leave a love bite against her knee, and brushed his five o'clock shadow against her inner thigh until she trembled at the sensation.

Cheeks still aflame, she rocked her head back and closed her eyes as his tongue dipped shallowly into her. His hands found her breasts and tugged on her sensitive nipples, and when she groaned, he rewarded her with a deeper thrust. Hard in and slow out, and she pressed forward with the delicious sensation.

That rumbling growl he always had ready was nothing shy of erotic as the vibrations went straight through her sex and into her belly. He jerked her hips forward like he couldn't get enough of her.

He was so fucking good at this.

Elbows locked, sheets clenched in her fists, she couldn't' help but look down at him as his head bobbed sensually between her legs. She was gasping his name and every muscle in her body quivered as each stroke of his tongue brought her closer to release. His hands grabbed her ass tighter, and his tongue drove deeper and the sound of him sipping her filled the room, and she was gone, floating off somewhere. Her orgasm pounded through her, pulsing, quickening as she ground out a curse at the shock of how hard her insides clenched around him.

Bron reached over and plucked the condom from the floor. Ripping paper sounded, but she hadn't the energy to do more than fall back onto the covers. Her bones had left her, and now she had no more substance than sand. Bron leaned over her with that sexy smile. Half of his face was shadowed, and half was lit by the bedside lamp and his eyes were so bright. He looked utterly full of himself and she couldn't help the giggle that bubbled from her throat.

"Soft curses and my name as nothing more than a whisper on your lips," he said low. "You'll have to do better than that, love."

"What do you want?"

He covered her with his body, his frame pressing her into the mattress. The head of his cock touched her right as the last aftershock faded.

His eyes grew serious and hungry. "I'm going to make you scream my name."

Oh, when he spoke like that, such a knot of anticipation filled her belly.

Another shallow thrust, and she could see it all so clearly. He was going to drive her mad with lust until she begged. Pressure was already building again as he pressed into her a little deeper. He was big and thick, and fuck the physics that seemed to say there was no way he could fit himself inside of her, she wanted all of him. To the base, to the hilt, she wanted him to push into her until there was no end and beginning to their connection.

She wanted to touch him.

Running her palms down his taut abdomen, she felt him flex with every thrust. He hadn't taken his gaze from her, and when she closed her eyes to absorb all the sensations he was pulling from her body, he cupped the sides of her face and tangled his fingers in her hair.

"No, Sam," he murmured. "I want to watch you."

Opening her eyes, she tipped her chin and kissed his lips. He tasted rich and heady, but she was already too far gone to be embarrassed by the taste of herself on him. Forcing his tongue past her lips once, twice, he eased back and bucked into her again, deeper.

"Tell me something no one else knows," he whispered.

Cupping his hands with her own to keep them in place against her face, she said, "You're my only." Only man to be invited to her bed. Only love. Only everything. "And you?"

"I love you," he rasped. "Always have, always will."

Closing her eyes to absorb the truth of his words, a tear of happiness fled the corner as he slowly pressed the entire length of his cock inside of her. He was long and thick, and she had to remind herself to relax or she wouldn't be able to take him, but the small pain of the stretch was worth the reward as he touched her clit. She gasped as pleasure shot through her, and he pulled back by inches before he drove in again, harder this time.

God, she'd missed this—missed him. Missed the feel of him inside of her. Arching against him, blow for blow, they bucked faster and faster until she was on the verge of spilling over again.

The sound of their skin hitting, the bed ramming against the wall, the constant rumble in his throat and his eyes...they'd be terrifying if she didn't know his heart. Their thrusting became frantic and his muscles strained, tensed, and she chanted a high-pitched wail of pleasure every time he filled her.

And he'd been right. He did make her scream his name as she came around him. Gritting his teeth, Bron froze, then thrust erratically into her as he found his own release.

They lay there for a long time, pulsing together, slower and slower until every aftershock was through.

He kissed her cheeks and her forehead and finally her lips, and lifted off her. Without a word, he curled her against his stomach and sighed the most contented sound.

What they'd done had just sealed her fate. She could feel it. No matter where she went now, or where she ended up, he would always be it for her.

"Bron?" she asked.

"Mmm?"

"I love you, too. Always have, always will."

TEN

A tingling in his arm woke Bron up. He tried to wiggle his fingers, but they were completely numb and he turned toward Samantha. She was asleep against his shoulder, her full lips slightly parted and her dark hair fanned out in rolling waves against the pillow. She looked at peace, like all of the stress of the past few days had lifted.

She'd been so open to trying new things with him. He'd always known she was brave, but last night had proved it. He could see her reservation about him tasting her, but she'd let him, and he'd felt the exact moment she let herself go.

God, she was beautiful.

As gently as he could, he lifted her head and freed

his arm.

It hadn't been like this with Muriel. She had hated him touching her. She slept in a separate bedroom after their first year together. Sometimes she had cried after they were intimate. Neither of them wanted that marriage, and they'd both suffered to make it work. He got it. Muriel was in love with someone else too and he was a poor substitute for him just as she was a poor substitute for Sam. Even understanding that she felt she was betraying the man she loved by sleeping with Bron didn't take the sting off of the fact that for years, a woman, his wife, had cringed when he touched her.

With Sam, everything was effortless.

Just the brush of his hand brought a shiver to her sometimes, and he relished in how her body reacted to him, how aroused she smelled, when he gave her affection. By the end of his marriage to Muriel, he was afraid of touching anyone—of seeing that disappointed look in anyone's face. But with Sam, he was learning to trust himself again. She was teaching him how to enjoy intimacy in a way he thought he'd never feel again.

Three more days wasn't enough.

He'd stupidly thought if he was sated with Sam this week, it would hold him—for a while at least. But the more he was with her, the more dire her presence felt to his happiness.

She's human.

Rocking upward, he sat on the edge of the bed and scrubbed his hands over his face.

His head knew last night was a mistake. But his heart didn't seem to give a shit.

Turning, he watched her make a sleep sound and reach out across his empty side.

His bear had chosen her last night. He'd as good as claimed her, and the only way to appease his beast was to be with her. It would cost him his place in the clan. It would cost him his rank and his friends. He wouldn't be allowed to come back here, and there would be no more sanctuary for him.

He would grow weak without the clan. Shifters were social creatures by nature, and he would be a rogue out amongst humans, always hiding what he was, always afraid of someone finding out. His bear was dominant and blood thirsty, and was happy with the challenges and battles that came with being second to the alpha. Here, he could fight a man to calm his beast, then take him out for a beer the next day. Away from Joseph, he couldn't blow off steam or someone would die.

His bear demanded he stay with his mate, but the price of him leaving here would eventually be his sanity.

Too caged feeling to stay in the small bedroom, he sauntered into the bathroom and flipped the light switch. With the water running full blast, he lifted his gaze to the mirror above the sink.

The glass there gave an unflattering reflection. His eyes were inhumanly light, and cold looking. The angles of his face were jagged and he looked tired despite having the best sleep he'd had in weeks. Gripping both sides of the sink, he gusted a breath of air.

If Samantha ever looked close enough at his pale skin, she'd be able to see the scars from his battle to the top. Faint silver slashes crisscrossed his torso and back, but humans didn't have eyesight like he did. They were so obvious to him. No, he wasn't vain, but his marred skin served as a reminder of the peril that encompassed his life.

Sam had no business bonding with a beast like

him.

He'd already dragged her into more danger than she could even imagine, and now the thought of something happening to her at the hands of his people gutted him.

The bedroom door creaked, and he could hear her soft footsteps down the hall. She was probably worried and coming to check on him. Leaving the door cracked, he cupped water and scrubbed his face in an attempt to dim the shifter brightness out of his eyes.

Sam screamed.

****

Samantha couldn't even tell what kind of animal it was. Most of its skin was missing and blood ran rivers across the new porch. The early dawn light illuminated the word *whore*, written in sticky crimson.

Another scream of horror bubbled up from her, and as she took a breath to shriek again, Bron clamped his hand over her mouth and pulled her inside.

"It's dead," she sobbed, clutching the elastic waist of his boxers. "Who would do that to an animal?"

Bron had hidden the dead creature completely from her sight by placing his wide shoulders between them, but she still saw it in her mind as clear as day. The little animal's lips had pulled back over its sharp teeth, like it was terrified in death.

"Fuck," he muttered.

"Who, Bron? Who would do this?"

"Sam, I need you to go inside. I have to do something."

"Bron, please." Her whisper was ragged. "Who?"

He turned and gripped her shoulders. "My people. It's old magic. They think they've cursed you but I'm going to fix it, okay? Go inside and wait for me. Make sure the back door and the windows are all locked."

Without waiting for her to answer, he stepped onto the porch and closed the door behind him. Out the window, she could see him bend over and pick up the creature by its tail in one swift motion and haul it to his truck. After he tossed it in the bed, he strode back to the house, muttering something too low for her to hear through the door. He crouched on the cracked pavement path and picked up a handful of soil, then scanned the yard. The wind lifted dirt from his grasp, throwing it to the west, and Bron's nostrils

181

flared.

His look darkened by the moment, and he picked up something from the yard too small for her to see. Lips pursed into a grim line, he hit the outside faucet and sprayed down the porch with the kinked old water hose, and Samantha went and checked the locks.

Fear pounded adrenaline through her veins and she couldn't stop shaking as she checked and rechecked the windows. Someone had come to her house, wrote that awful word in some defenseless animal's blood and knocked on her door to make sure she saw it. She thought it was Dillon and the crew here early for their shift.

Bron had called them *his people*. How could he claim to be part of a group who would do such a horrific thing?

The front door creaked open and Bron walked in with his cell phone pressed to his ear. It must've been in his truck all night. "Two minutes? Yeah, I hear you. Don't leave her until I get back." He clicked the phone closed, and locked the door behind him.

His gaze only landed on her for a second before a frown furrowed his brows and he ducked around her toward the bathroom.

"More mysteries?" She knew where this was going and was already pissed. "Now there's dead animals and curses and black magic?"

"Not black magic," he said, hitting the tap in the bathroom and washing the red off his hands. "Old magic."

Rubbing her eyes, she moaned, "What does that even mean? What's the difference?"

"It's complicated."

"Isn't everything with you?"

"Dillon is going to be here in a minute, and I need you to stay here with him and the boys until I get back. I'll only be gone a couple of hours."

"You gonna go un-curse me?" she spat out. "And your people are dicks, by the way. A whore? Really? I bet that isn't in your witchy culty old magic books. That word sounds pretty friggin' modern to me."

"Sam," he rumbled. "Don't let this ruin what we had last night. It's not a big deal. I'll handle it."

"Oh, last night. You mean the part where you said you loved me, but this morning you're still stacking secrets between us." Her voice faltered and her lip trembled. "You'll never let me in, will you?"

It hit her then. It didn't matter if she stayed three days or for eternity. There would always be walls too thick and too high for her to ever hurdle to get to him. He didn't know how to love. Not like she deserved.

His eyes burned with fury as he turned and leaned back against the sink. "I can't be what you want, Sam. I can't answer the questions you want answered. I'm trying my best here and I'm wading through waters I've never navigated before. I'll be back soon." He left her trailing behind him to the front door, and at the last moment before he shut her in, he turned. "Trust Dillon, Grant and Reese, and no one else. You hear?"

Too furious to speak, she nodded once, and the door slammed behind him.

He was a jack-hole-dick-wagon for leaving her completely in the dark. Maybe she should leave Joseph now. He had warned her she was in trouble, but it hadn't seemed real until someone left a dead animal on her porch. Now she was scared. Real scared.

A knock on the door made her jump, but it was just Dillon and Grant. The third crewmember, the giant one she'd never caught his name, wasn't with them today.

"Heard you had some drama," Dillon said when she opened the door.

"Someone left a dead animal on my front porch."

"What did it look like?" he asked, setting down a bucket with a bunch of tools inside.

"I don't know. It had been skinned, but it had sharp teeth, little pink toes and a tail."

"Opossum," he and Grant said at the same time.

"Whoo," Grant called over his shoulder as he hauled a giant box on a dolly into the kitchen. "You pissed someone off good, didn't you? Hot water heater is in, so I'm going to be in here for an hour. Holler if you need me." The box clanged as he set it down and opened a closet door.

"Dillon, do you know anything about this? Who would be dropping a dead animal on the stoop of my house?"

"You have to take that up with your mate, darlin'. I've got orders to stay zip-lipped, and I'm not pissing Bron off again. He'll bleed me."

"Mate?"

Dillon tipped his chin and narrowed his eyes. His fair hair fell out of his eyes and back as he studied her with a calculating look. "See? You already have me all turned upside down. I'm not talking to you anymore. And if you tell Bron I said that, we're not friends anymore."

"Dillon."

"I mean it, Young. And I'm a good friend to have. I share my food and listen to boring girly shit with minimal whining, and I haven't even stolen any of those sexy panties you leave lying around everywhere."

"Oh, God, just stop talking. I won't tell him." She made a mental note to clean up any clothes she left lying around while she was at it, now that his temptation to pocket lingerie was out on the table.

Two hours of ignoring her completely, and the house was starting to feel too quiet. Dillon said he needed to be able to hear if someone was coming, so she wasn't allowed to even drown the silence in old classical songs. Really, it just sounded like he didn't want her to crank the volume because he didn't appreciate her taste in music.

She spent the early morning hours sweeping the floors, painting trim and ripping up the rest of the battered linoleum flooring in the kitchen. And when her stomach finally felt solid enough to eat something, she munched on a bagel and read a flyer Clean-It-Right Maid Service had left rubber-banded to her front door.

Anything to keep her mind from revisiting that poor dead animal.

Grant's phone rang and he stood and wiped his hands on an oily rag hanging from his pocket.

"Yeah?"

A muffled sound came from the other end, and she wished for supersonic dog hearing, because Grant was actually frowning. She'd never seen Grant frown. He was quiet, sure, but he usually had a smile, or at least a look of contentment on his tanned face. His dark eyes looked troubled when he handed her the phone.

"Hello?" she asked.

"Hey." Damn it was good to hear Bron's voice, even if she was still a little angry at the secrets he kept. "I'll be longer than I thought. I'm going to grab some stuff from my place so I can stay with you until Saturday. Are you all right?"

"Yes, I'm fine. Just really confused on how I'm supposed to handle all of this. I hate being left in the dark, and this all feels like a really, really big deal."

"It'll be okay." He sounded so somber right now, and she wished she could see what color his eyes were. Usually they seemed to change hues when he sounded like this. "I took care of the person who put the animal on your porch. It was the woman who pulled your hair at the meeting. She won't be doing that again. Hand me back over to Grant so I can tell him what needs to be done on the house today."

Grant had been leaning over the table, intensely watching her face, and he reached for the phone before Bron was even done speaking, like he could hear the conversation or something. These boys were weird.

"Uh, huh," Grant muttered into the cell. "Okay, got it." He paced around for a while, agreeing into the phone, and then he said, "And you're sure you want me to bring her to you right now. Like, right this minute?"

Well, that perked her right up.

"Okay, you got it, boss." He hung up the phone and pocketed it. "Hey, D. Bron wants us to take Samantha to his place."

Dillon peeked his head out of the back room.

"What? He said to stay here."

"I know, man, but he just told me he wants us to bring her to his house."

"Did he say why?"

"No. He just told me a list of shit a mile long that we have to do today, and then said right now, he wants us to bring her to him."

"Hmm," Dillon grunted with a frown. "Okay. Sam, you ready to go?"

Did he consider paint in her hair, no make-up, and holey jeans splattered with Carriage House green ready to go? "Yep."

"Thata girl. I'll drive."

Grant muttered, "Dick," and Samantha followed them out, careful to lock the door behind her lest some creepy blood-cursing witch cult decided to hold a séance in there while she was out.

She'd once bemoaned that nothing interesting ever happened in the sleepy town of Joseph, and now she wished she could be so naive again. How would she ever be able to explain anything that had happened here to Margie when she got back to Portland? Normal people didn't deal with dark threats and dead animals and late-night town cult meetings.

Her life had turned into a horror movie since she'd picked up Reese's call.

Being squished between two sexy giants would've been a dream come true last week, but now she felt claustrophobic. Something about the people here stifled the air, made it thicker and kicked up instincts she couldn't understand. Twenty minutes of bouncing around between their linebacker shoulders like a squishy pinball and she was ready to hurl herself out the open window. Thankfully, Dillon turned onto a familiar driveway and a quarter of a mile later, Bron's house came into view.

"Hey, remember that night you hid in the woods dressed like Catwoman and we busted you?" Dillon asked with an obnoxious smile.

She wanted to claw it off his face for reminding her. Even now, her face burned with the heat of embarrassment. "I wasn't dressed like Catwoman," she muttered. "I was dressed in spy clothes. Obviously."

"You're trouble," he said, pulling to a stop near Bron's truck and an unfamiliar silver jeep. "I like that."

She pushed Grant's shoulder, encouraging him to get the fuck out of her way so she could breathe, and stumbled out of the bronco after him.

He led her up the porch stairs and barged through the door without knocking. Rude.

"What are you doing here?" Bron asked from the bottom of the stairs where he sat with his arms draped over his knees. His eyes were wide with confusion, and a woman slowly stood from a couch in the living room.

Samantha recognized her dark hair and light green eyes from the funeral reception. Muriel.

"What are *you* doing here?" Samantha asked, trying to stifle the jealous rage that slashed up her spine.

"I told you, I'm packing so I can stay at your place without having to make another trip out here."

"This isn't what it looks like," Muriel said, her delicate eyebrows knitted with concern. Probably fake concern. Samantha wanted to kick her in the vagina.

"Wait, what?" Bron turned to Muriel. "What does this look like?" Suspicion grew on his face and his nostrils flared as the breeze picked up through the open door behind them. "Samantha, why are you here? Seriously."

"Because you told Grant to bring me." What, Lying Shit for Brains had amnesia too?

"No. I told Grant all the work that needed to be done, and then I hung up." His eyes slid to Grant and turned cold as ice. "You sack of shit."

"I'm under orders," Grant explained meekly, voice shaking.

"Whose?" Bron barked as he stood. His voice echoed against the walls of the cabin, and the sound made Samantha hunch into herself.

"I'm sorry, man. She has to go for the good of the clan. You know it. You can see it, you just don't want it to be true." Grant's voice dipped lower as he turned sad, dark eyes to her. "I'm sorry, Sam. He's a Cress."

Like that explained anything. She was perfectly aware of Bron's last name.

Grant had betrayed her somehow, but hell if she knew what that meant. Did he want her to see Bron with Muriel? Okay, that sucked, but it didn't account for Dillon rearing back and punching Grant in his dumbfounded weasel face.

A tremendous crash rattled the house and

Samantha covered her ears with her hands. Outside, all three vehicles had been pushed over and were still rocking. Shattered glass covered the lawn, and a streak of fur bolted past the doorway.

Something monstrous was outside.

"Oh, my God!" she screamed in terror as she lunged to close the door.

Dillon was pummeling Grant, who wasn't moving anymore, and Bron grabbed her hand before she reached the door.

"They're coming," Bron said in a tone so quiet, his words sent shards of ice through her veins.

ELEVEN

"We have to get you to the main road," Bron said.

"How do we get to the road? There's a monster out there and the cars are upside down in the fucking yard!" Samantha was growing hysterical, but an utter adrenaline dump had flooded her system and she was ready for fight or flight. Either would do right now.

"What should I do?" Muriel asked in a rush. "I can help."

"No, you can't and this isn't your fight. They aren't after you. Go home. Dillon, he's out. Leave him."

Dillon's eyes had gone dead, but he stopped pummeling Grant and followed them with a look of grim acceptance.

Dragging Samantha through the kitchen, Bron

flipped open his phone and hit a speed dial number. "Reese, Sam's in trouble. I need you at my place now. Right now. They've come for her." He hung up the phone and yanked the back door open.

Dillon followed close behind and took his shirt off. Oh, dear goodness, that awful sobbing sound was coming from her. Dillon was all abs and arms and seriousness and why the hell was he chippendaling it when there was a giant furry monster hunting them?

Samantha's breath came in pants and she balked when Bron led her outside. "We should stay in the house. That thing is out here."

"The house won't stop them. We have to get you to the road and headed back toward town. They can't get you there. Not like this."

"Them? Like more than one of those things?"

"Four at least, maybe five, but it'll be okay. Dillon and I are here, and Reese will be here soon."

She was crying as he dragged her toward the tree line. His hand was strong and steady, dry and warm, while hers was clamming up more with every step they took away from the safety of the house. That thing upended three cars. No, not cars. A jeep, a bronco, and a jacked-up pickup truck. What chance did four people have against something like that?

The hairs prickled on her neck and when she turned around, Dillon was gone. "Dillon?" she whimpered.

"He's fine," Bron said in a strange, gravelly voice. "He's flanking us."

Alder, spruce, pine and fir towered above them as they weaved through the woods. A roar echoed through the trees, long and loud, and she dug her nails into his hand. "What was that?"

"A bear," Bron said, void of emotion.

A bear? A mother fucking bear? She couldn't breathe, couldn't move, and she was going to pass out with the breakneck pace Bron was setting. Her legs locked against the forward motion.

With a grunt, Bron turned and pulled her into his arms, and continued on his way.

"We should climb a tree," she suggested in a small, panicked voice.

"Bears can climb trees. You need to get to the—"

"Road. I get it."

Another roar followed by a couple of short bursts sounded from much closer. And she buried her face against Bron's chest. His heart was racing, and that scared her more than anything. It had been easier to pretend she was going to be okay when Bron seemed so confident, but maybe that was all an act.

He began to jog as they ran parallel to the meadow in front of the house. His strides were long and graceful, like she weighed nothing. Holding on tighter, she cast a glance behind him and gasped.

A giant black furred bear was charging full speed for them.

"Bron?"

"I hear him."

"Bron?" she asked again in a higher octave.

"Dillon's got him."

A grizzly rushed from the trees and tackled the other. End over end they tumbled and a scream of terror burst out of her. Bron clamped his hand over her mouth.

"You'll bring them all right to us if you show that kind of fear, and we need them spaced out. Can you run?"

"There's two bears," she said dumbly. "There's two bears fighting."

She couldn't take her eyes from the frenzied violence. It wasn't play fighting over a blackberry

197

bush. These animals were battling to kill each other.

"Can you run?" Bron clipped out again.

"Yes," she whispered.

Setting her down, he pulled his shirt over his head as they ran side by side.

"What are you doing?"

"Keep running." His eyes were so serious when they met hers. They were so light, her breath caught in her throat. "Don't stop and don't look back, no matter what."

A loud crash and crunching metal sounded from back by the house, and she lifted her shoulders to her ears and crouched as she stumbled through the brush.

Crashing trees sounded and two more bears, one ruddy and one dirty blonde charged from the east.

"Go!" Bron yelled. "Don't look back."

But his words had turned gravelly and strange sounding, and she couldn't *not* look.

Heaving breath, she tossed a glance over her shoulder and skidded to a stop. Bron's spine rippled from the base to his shoulders, and he grew massive as dark chestnut colored fur sprouted from him. His face elongated with a spattering of sick sounding crunches and he dropped to all fours as six inch claws stabbed through his hands. And when he stood again, just a moment after he'd been the man she loved, he wasn't human anymore, but a towering, eleven-foot grizzly bear.

Her screams were covered by his bellowing roar as he charged the two bears.

This wasn't real. It wasn't! It couldn't be. It went against science and nature and probably every other law that governed how the world turned. Frozen in terror and panting like a racehorse as tears streamed down her face, Samantha turned to see another bear charging straight for her. And this time, there were no bear people to save her.

She had to save herself.

Spinning, she ran as fast as her legs could carry her, stumbling and righting herself and leaping through thin areas in the brush, hoping to slow it down. From the crashing foliage that was growing closer with every step, she was failing.

There wasn't time to look back. There wasn't time to lose her footing, only to put one foot in front of the other faster than the last step. Branches whipped at her face and arms, and she sobbed when the bear roared so close to her it hurt her eardrums.

Another bear was running at her up ahead, trapping her. It was smaller and black, and when Samantha looked it in the face, the bear wasn't focused on her, but on the animal behind her.

It was stupid—so stupid—but she couldn't help the terrified wish that came from her throat. "Reese?"

Long white teeth flashed as the bear grunted, and Samantha had no choice but to hope this one was on her side. At the last second, she veered off to the left and the black bear lunged at the one behind her.

Samantha's throat was raw from screaming but that didn't stop her from giving it another go. Bears and people. People bears. Joseph was full of them, and she'd been living as a naive human all these years.

And Bron...nothing he'd ever told her was true.

Running, stumbling, crying, Samantha didn't even know the direction of the road anymore. She couldn't think over the echoing slaps and bellows of pain that shook the woods. As she burst through the tree line and into a clearing near the driveway, the silver jeep nearly ran her over. At the near miss, Muriel slammed on the brakes to the damaged vehicle and ushered her in.

"Are you one of them? Are you trying to kill me?" Even to her own ears, Samantha sounded frightened and at the edge of sanity.

"Yes and no. I have no reason to kill you. This isn't my fight, remember? Now get in before one of them comes for you."

"Bron said only trust Dillon, Grant and Reese."

The woman's gaze flicked over her shoulder. "Grant betrayed you. I won't. I'll explain what's happening if you get in. I don't want you dead, Samantha. You're the only one who can save me."

Samantha dared a glance behind her, and a blonde grizzly was running through the woods.

"I can get you to safety," Muriel tried again. "Now get in!"

Sprinting around the front, she dove onto the passenger seat, and Muriel hit the gas just as the bear reached them. The jeep was one of those off-road vehicles, with no doors and a soft fabric top that had been clipped back. Not exactly good at keeping bear claws from reaching in and snuffing out her life.

Muriel shifted gears and frowned at the rearview mirror. Samantha didn't even want to see how close the bear was. Metal crunched in the back and she clung to the seat for dear life as they weaved, spinning gravel this way and that. Muriel hit another gear and jammed the gas.

Swerving onto the main road, the woman huffed a relieved sound and Samantha dared a glance back. The bear stood on the side of the road, tilted his head to the sun and bellowed.

"We aren't allowed in town in our bear forms," Muriel explained over the engine noise. "That's as far as they can go until they change back."

"Bron is a bear," she said. "He's a bear. A real bear with fur and claws."

"Don't freak out," Muriel said.

"Oh my gosh," Samantha said, rubbing her eyes until they hurt. "I slept with a bear. That's against the law, isn't it? I'm a criminal. I'm a sexual deviant."

"He's already slept with you?"

"Oh my gosh, I'm sorry. That was completely messed up to say in front of his wife."

"Ex-wife and it was never a real marriage. Do you love him?"

"Bron is a bear," she repeated. No matter how many times she said it, her mind couldn't get a grasp on the combination of words that had become an overwhelming truth in her life. Her stomach dropping to the floorboard beneath her feet. "I think I'm going to be sick." She swallowed hard and the churning only got worse as another mile passed. "Yep, I'm definitely going to be sick. Pull over."

Two hundred yards away from the safety of her own house, Samantha yacked in the bushes of Bethany Brown's house. Or at least it used to be Mrs. Brown's house before Samantha moved away, and from the perfect line of tulips she heaved onto, she was going to go out on a limb and say the notoriously fickle gardener was still queen of this roost.

Muriel gathered Samantha's long tresses at the base of her neck and rubbed her back. "I used to hate you," she whispered. She sounded so sad. "Bron loved you. Couldn't stop loving you no matter how hard he tried and no matter how hard I tried to make him. He used to say your name when he was with me—called me Sam by accident. But now I'm sad about what our marriage did to both of you. I didn't want this either. I had someone else I wanted too."

Samantha's shoulders shook as she held her stomach and hunched forward. Her heart was breaking. She hadn't known Bron at all. "Why did you help me back there?"

"My father is trying to force a reconciliation with Bron."

Samantha looked up, and the sun behind Muriel glowed through her hair, making a halo. "And you don't want that?"

"No. We worked hard for our divorce and neither one of us wants to go back to pretending. That's why I've been calling him. That's why I went over to his house today, so that we could figure out a way to avoid falling into the same vicious cycle. I can't choose another mate until Bron isn't an option for me anymore."

"You mean until he chooses me?"

Muriel nodded, and sadness pooled so deeply in her mossy hued eyes.

"What if he's hurt out there? And Dillon and Reese?"

"Bron will be fine. He's second in the clan and has fought almost every bear to get there. He's a brawler. Don't spare your concern for him in a shifter fight, Samantha."

She noticed Muriel didn't mention Dillon and

Reese though.

Muriel leaned closer. "You can't have him human."

Samantha's breath was shaking so badly, and she clutched her arms tighter around her middle to steady the tremors. "What do you mean?"

"It's not allowed. There are only seventy-five bear shifters left in the world and we can't breed with humans. It doesn't work."

"That's why they want me dead. His...clan?"

"He's a Cress—the last of the Cress line now that Trent is gone. His family ruled our kind a long time ago. He isn't allowed to mate an un-breedable female or he'll be banished, and you'll be in danger for always. And if he decides to leave with you, it will cost him his people, his place, the safety of his clan, everything."

"So he was never mine to begin with," Samantha murmured, defeated. She couldn't ask him to forsake everything for her. Hell, she didn't even know if he was what she wanted anymore. The lies had stacked up too tall between them. She would've understood when they were kids, if he would've let her in. But he'd chosen not to.

Muriel's voice dipped to a whisper. "I can turn you if it's what you want, but you should think about it first. It is risky, and painful, and it can't be undone."

She tried to imagine turning into the thing Bron had been, and her mind skittered away in fear. She'd watched his bones break and claws rip from his flesh. How could she ever willingly do that to herself? "If you can turn people, why are there so few of you left?"

"Because the clans have forgotten how. The women in my family are medicine people though, and the books have passed to me."

"I think I need to leave."

Muriel was quiet for a long time, then offered Samantha a hand and helped her up. "Maybe you should. It's your best shot at survival."

She drove Samantha the last stretch to her house and scribbled her number on a piece of paper before handing it to her. "In case you ever decide he's worth it."

"Thanks," Samantha said, as soft as the breeze, then turned before Muriel could see the devastation in her face.

She loved him more than anything, but this was

her humanity she was talking about snuffing out. After all she'd been through, she couldn't think about anything but the moment Bron changed into an animal, over and over on an endless loop.

She had to get away from here.

Jogging up the walkway, she pushed her way inside and threw her things haphazardly into the suitcase. Tears fell onto her tossed clothes in a steady river of pain, but fuck it all, she'd just watched the people she loved fighting as creatures she'd only heard about in legends.

And worst was all the lies.

Lies, lies, lies—her life had been peppered with them and she didn't know what to believe now.

It would be impossible to think clearly about all of this in Hells Canyon. She needed to be out in the real world, with other humans, if she wanted to get a grasp on what had happened here.

Overwhelmed and scared, she threw her luggage in the back of her Jetta and peeled down the road that led out of town.

Bron was a bear shifter. Her friends were shifters too, and she'd been kept in the dark all her life. Oh, what stories they must have strung together to keep her naive. How many times had they shared secret jokes at her expense, and met behind her back.

What an idiot she must've looked like to them.

Tears burned her eyes as she blasted past the *Now Leaving Joseph, Oregon* sign, and she dashed them away with the back of her hand.

She had been trustworthy, they just hadn't wanted to let her in.

And she'd be damned if she was going to live her life feeling like an outsider.

TWELVE

Samantha hadn't known where she was going until she hit the Benton county border. Her thoughts had swirled around and around the impossible things she'd seen, and now she was questioning everything.

Like how Dad was involved in this and how much he knew about Bron's people. Suddenly, it seemed really important she talk to him about what really happened when she was younger.

One quick phone call to the prison and she was told she would have to wait until tomorrow to visit Dad.

And as impatient as she was, she thought perhaps it was better this way. She needed some time to regain control over her emotions, and to think about what had happened today. Already, a hundred strange occurrences from her past had clicked into place with the explanation that Joseph was overrun with paranormal creatures. She needed time to marinate on all of this before she walked into that prison demanding answers like a deranged lunatic.

About ten miles from the prison was a hole-in-the-wall hotel called Comfy Nights Motel. The welcome sign looked to be about a hundred years old and some of the letters were missing. The parking lot was cracked and resembled a map of chaotic Portland streets, and there looked to be only ten rooms in the flat-roofed, dilapidated building. But at thirty bucks a night, if it was good enough for her budget, it was good enough for her.

Evening stretched long shadows across the sleepy town by the time she was checked in and picked her room. Lucky number seven, because her life didn't need any more bad mojo right now.

Settled into the musty smelling room, she ordered Chinese delivery and ate her weight in egg rolls, dousing her heartache in calories and soy sauce.

Flopping back onto the bed, she stared at the beige ceiling and sniffled. Her tears had dried up in the car on the long drive over here. She had frightened the cashier at a gas station when she'd come in to pay for gas and an economy sized package of chocolate cupcakes. Her eyes were red and puffy, and she probably resembled a weepy demon when she'd handed him her crumbled twenty dollar bill, but so what? She wouldn't ever see him again. At least he didn't make the sign of the cross when she left.

The ripple of Bron's spine played again in her mind. This is why he growled during intimacy, and why his eyes changed colors. That hadn't been a figment of her imagination that they lightened. It was probably why he insisted on wearing sunglasses all the damned time.

If she went back, would he do that still? Now that she knew?

They'd been star-crossed lovers all this time, and she hadn't even known. If he could keep something so huge a secret for so long, how could she ever trust him to tell her everything? That's what she wanted with a man. Complete trust. Bron hiding this huge part of his life, perhaps the biggest part of it, made her think he wasn't trustworthy at all.

Her thoughts turned back to the night Dad had come back covered in the blood of Bron's father.

The soft murmur of her parents talking—no, arguing—woke Samantha up from a deep sleep. It was finals week and junior year had been hard on her grades. She had an English test first period and couldn't be losing sleep because her parents were at it again.

Pissed off and sleepy, she flung her feet from the bed and padded down the hallway.

"What have you done, Tommy?" Momma asked as tears welled up in her eyes.

The sight of Dad drew Samantha up short, and she crouched in the shadows of the dark hall. From his fingertips to his elbows, he was covered in sticky looking crimson. "I did what I had to do."

"Is he dead?" Momma's voice came out a frightened, high-pitched sound. "You were supposed to scare him, not kill him!"

Dad brushed past Momma and the kitchen sink turned on full blast. Samantha imagined all that red swirling down the drain.

"We have to tell her why," Momma whispered.

"Why you did this, and why he deserved it."

"No! She never finds out, or what I did was for nothing."

Samantha dared a peek around the corner. Her dad, tall and dark headed to contrast with Momma's petit blonde, was standing with his back to her, scrubbing and washing his arms like he'd never feel clean again.

Momma rested her hand against his back. "Oh, Tommy. What'll we do?"

"You'll get her out of here—away from Joseph as soon as you can. Don't look back. Don't let Sam look back either."

She couldn't stand it anymore, hiding in the shadows when down to her marrow she felt like her life was being blasted out of a canon. She couldn't leave Joseph. Leaving Joseph meant leaving Bron, and the thought was simply beyond her.

"What did you do?" she asked as she stepped into the living room.

Dad started and turned. "How long have you been there?"

"Long enough. Who did you hurt?" Samantha's eyes were wide and she felt like she had swallowed jagged

213

ice.

A pounding sounded at the door and Momma shrieked.

"Open up, it's the police."

Dad turned a somber gaze to Momma and kissed her cheeks, her forehead, and lingered on her lips. "I love you, Charlene. No matter what, I'll always love you."

Then he strode past where Samantha was hovered and hesitated with his hand on the door. With an agonized look over his shoulder at her, he said, "I'm sorry."

"Tommy Young?" an officer asked as soon as Dad opened the door.

"Yes."

"You're under arrest for the murder of Daniel Cress."

"No," Samantha said in horror. "No!" she screamed as Momma caught her. "You son of a bitch! Why?"

Mr. Cress was dead and there was no discernable reason why Dad would do such a vile thing. That was Bron's father's blood on her daddy's arms. The same arms he'd used to lift her up as a baby. The same arms that had tucked her in at night until she was twelve.

The same arms that hugged her after report cards came in.

She was going to be sick.

"Momma, why?" she wailed as the sheriff and his two deputies dragged Dad off to a waiting police cruiser. Lights blared red and blue, casting the house in an eerie glow.

Momma was sobbing, and between hiccups, she said, "He had to, honey. He just felt he had to."

Dad had never liked Bron, or her relationship with him, but that was no reason to kill someone. Maybe this was some desperate move to break her and Bron apart. Surely he couldn't love her still if she was family to the murderer of his father.

Bron. Bron's father was dead.

Struggling from Momma's grasp, she snatched the keys from the table and rushed to the old station wagon parked in the driveway. Pulling through the yard and around the police car where they were lowering Dad's head into it, she sped down the two streets that separated her and Bron's house.

More patrol cars were parked every which way around his small home, and yellow tape was being put up around the woods out back. Trent and Bron sat on the front porch, talking to an officer, Trent with his head in his hands and his shoulders shaking like he was crying, and Bron looking stoically ahead and answering questions.

She froze in the yard, afraid to approach and see the hatred that would surely be there in his eyes.

Bron turned slowly, but the hatred wasn't there. Only deep sadness and pain. He stood and ignored a question the officer asked. Stepping from the porch as if he was on autopilot, he didn't slow down as he approached.

Running, she threw herself into him, and he caught her and squeezed until her ribs felt like they would break.

"I'm sorry he did this. I'm sorry, I'm sorry," she chanted, wishing her words could take away some of Bron's pain.

He buried his face in the hollow between her shoulder and throat, but he wasn't crying. He never cried. It wasn't his way to show emotion like that. Instead, he asked against her neck, "Are you okay?"

What? Of course she wasn't okay. Dad was a murderer and her life was breaking apart like shards of splintering bone. Everyone in town would hate her.

But tonight wasn't about the destruction her father had caused to her life. It was about Bron, because his mom packed up and left years ago, and now his daddy was dead. And she couldn't help but feel it was her fault somehow.

"Are you?" she asked, easing back and cupping his face.

The grim emptiness in his eyes was answer enough. He might never be okay again.

She'd gone so long despising Dad for ruining everything, for the guilt that she had carried that she somehow should've known how messed up he was and stopped him. Momma had held onto the belief that Dad was still a good man, but no matter what she said to convince Samantha, she couldn't erase the memories of his arms drenched in another man's blood.

College hadn't been an option after Momma got sick, and Dad was rotting away behind bars while Samantha watched her only remaining family wither away to nothing.

He hadn't been there because of his violent decision.

She'd cursed him when Momma had called out his name at the end. He'd chosen not to be present in their lives, and she'd never known why. Maybe she never would.

Unless he felt like explaining what really happened tomorrow at visitation, she could go to her grave wondering why her soft-spoken father decided to turn killer on a man she'd eaten Sunday dinner with for as long as she'd been able to remember.

Samantha sighed miserably. Everything was so messed up, and it all seemed to revolve around her lifelong bond with Bron.

Maybe that was it.

Perhaps her relationship with him wasn't the natural order for her life. How could it be? He wasn't even human. And everything around them had gone so wrong as they cleaved onto each other tighter.

And then Bron had been the first to give into fate by marrying Muriel, while her stubborn heart threw a joyous middle finger at destiny and made it impossible to find a normal man, or even a normal relationship.

She'd been motionless for six years, like some prehistoric animal frozen into a glacier.

She should run as far away from Bron and his people as she could and never look back. It was important to her survival that she find a life somewhere else.

But the thought of never seeing him again, even after realizing what he was, slashed jagged pain through her middle until she curled in on herself on the threadbare hotel room comforter.

With either decision, she lost something vital.

****

Inhaling deeply, Samantha looked up at the ceiling tiles as she stood like a star and got patted down by a handsy guard with coffee breath and sour disposition written all over his face.

"Turn around," he clipped out.

She did and, "Oh!" Her backside got a firm grab, both cheeks. A metal wand that made little clicking noises was brushed up and down her, and she was herded with the other prison visitors to a waiting room with several tables.

The prison wasn't a big one, and altogether there were twelve people visiting inmates today. Samantha sank onto a bench seat and scanned the room. She'd only been here one time with Momma when Dad was first assigned here after the trial, and after that, she'd refused to come. It looked just like she remembered it. White walls, white tile floors that squeaked under her shoes, metal tables and seats. Cold and lonely and she wished she had thought to bring a jacket to ward off the chill this place induced.

Her hands shook like they always did when she was nervous, so she clenched them and frowned at the clock incased in a miniature prison of bars. It was five 'til one, and the fluttering nerves in her stomach were beginning to make her feel queasy.

At a table nearby, a woman with dark hair and matching lipstick tried to quiet a squalling baby, and on the other side was an elderly couple, probably there to visit their son. This place was all filled up with sad stories.

She wasn't the only one who'd had a rough go of it. The crying child beside her might very well grow up without a father, and the parents beside her probably had such hopes for their boy when he was a child.

Inmates filed in and sat across from their loved ones. Hugging wasn't allowed, and she stood when she saw the man who vaguely resembled Dad. His hair was completely streaked with gray now, and deep wrinkles etched into his face. An intricate tattoo snaked up his neck, and his thin lips curved up in a tentative smile when he saw her.

"Nice ink," she said, sitting down as he took the seat across from her.

"Got it when your mom died. My roommate did it for me before he got out. I have a new roommate now." The glint of happiness he had worn when he'd seen her drained away. "He's not as nice." Clasping his hands in front of him on the table, he leveled her a look. "I told you to leave Joseph."

"How did you know I was there in the first place?"

His expression became hard, and she could see him closing down completely. He reminded her of Bron with all of his carefully guarded secrets. Ridiculous men.

"I know, so cut the shit with me, Dad."

Shooting a warning glance at the guard who stood in the doorway of the room, he leaned forward and murmured, "Know what?"

Canting her head, she tried to still the fury that was surging through her. She was so damned tired of everyone keeping everything from her. Inhaling through her nose, she exhaled a steadying breath and licked her lips. "Bear."

Dad made a clicking sound and shook his head like he was disgusted. "Bron promised. You were supposed to have a normal life and go on to find someone who suited you."

"Except I couldn't, because I didn't know how much danger I was in. You knew back then, didn't you?" She straightened her spine and glared at him, his amber-colored eyes older, masculine versions of hers. "Dad, I swore I would die before I asked you again, but I have to know. What happened with Mr. Cress that night? And don't bullshit me and give me some other mystery to solve. Just be straight with me. For once, I just need someone to tell me the truth."

"He was going to kill you, Sam," Dad whispered. "Bron was next in line to lead, and his daddy didn't want you in the way. Bron told me Daniel's plans because he didn't know what else to do. I tried to reason with Daniel that night. I told him I'd take you away and we'd never come back, but he said you and Bron had bonded as good as a mated pair and you two would find your way back to each other, no matter what I did." His breath hitched and he leaned back. "So I killed him. That was the choice I made to keep you safe, and I'd do it again to see you like this. Strong and grown up. And smart as a whip, like you were from a little baby. Screw Daniel Cress and what you thought you knew about him. He was going to hurt you, and I would die ten times over before I let that happen."

Her face crumpled and she looked down as twin tears fled to her cheeks and made pit-pat sounds on the cold metal table. "Why didn't you just tell me?" she asked in a broken whisper.

"Because you'd defend me. You would bring too much attention to this and out every last one of Bron's people, and most of them aren't bad people. They're trying to make it just like everybody else, and Joseph is their last safe haven. I murdered a man. Doesn't matter the reason, I'm accepting my consequences. And hopefully in a few years, I'll get out and visit your momma's grave and maybe see if you have time for a dinner date with your old man. It won't be the life I had, but it'll be something, and it'll be worth it because you are alive. I know what splitting up has done to you and Bron. I can see it when he comes to visit me, and your momma said you acted the same before she passed. I used to love her like that—like you two love each other." His voice cracked on the last word and he cleared his throat and blinked rapidly. "I know how hard this must be, and I'm sorry it has to be this way, but there are rules. You can't be together. You just have to find a way to move on."

"And if I can't?" Her weak words came out quiet and airy as her throat tightened around her emotions.

"You have to. You're a survivor. It's in your blood."

"One minute," the guard at the door called out.

"Sam, there's a journal in the house. It'll explain the things I can't here. Under the carpet in my old closet, there is a loose floorboard. Pull it up and it'll make up for all the things I hid from you. It'll tell you where you come from."

"Time," said the guard, and the other inmates rose from their seats.

"I'm sorry, Sam. I'm so sorry," Dad said as a tear tracked down his cheek. Roughly, he thumbed it away and walked out with the others. He looked back just as he disappeared behind the door, and his hard look was back in place again.

THIRTEEN

Samantha gripped the steering wheel in a steely grasp that hurt her knuckles. The rain was relentless as she leaned forward and tried to keep her car in the right lane. The lines were barely visible.

Everything she'd thought had been wrong, and now her entire life was turned upside down. She'd spent so much energy hating a man who'd sacrificed everything he had to save her life. And for no other reason than he was her dad, and he loved her.

Joseph looked like a ghost town, probably due to the torrential downpour, and she passed just one other car on the road. It was an old classic car with rust on the fender.

In her driveway, she wrestled her suitcase out of

the trunk, then ran for the door. The temptation to see Bron again was great, but her need to find out what Dad was talking about outweighed it by ounces. If she saw him now, he'd clam up on her, and it would hurt, and she needed to be at her strongest if she was going to sift through the mysteries her father had bestowed upon her today.

The light switch didn't work, and when she looked out the window, none of the other houses had lights on either. Power must be out in this part of the grid.

Clicking on her multi-tool light, she peeled off her soaking wet jacket and strode to her parents old room in the back of the house. Her boots made hollow sounds against the floorboards, which looked to be newly stained. Work hadn't ceased in her absence, which meant Bron and Dillon were just fine after the battle. She knew Reese was okay because when Samantha clicked on her cell phone this afternoon, she had four missed calls from her, and a voicemail checking to see if she was okay.

Was she okay? She just found out werebears existed. That answer was *hell no*.

In the closet, she pointed the tiny flashlight in one

corner, then the other, and wiggled her finger under a frayed carpet edge. Pulling harder, she yanked it back to reveal dusty wooden floors. Scrabbling against the edges, she dislodged a plank and pulled an ancient looking leather-bound journal from its depths.

A folded piece of paper fell out, and she sat against the wall and unfolded it.

Dear Sam,

If you've found this, it means something has happened to me which prevents me from telling you about the culture you were born into. Traditionally, the sons and daughters in our lineage have been told about their responsibilities on their twenty-first birthdays, but the custom has been lost over the years as the families we are bound to protect have died out.

You are a Hunter, my dear girl, as I am, and as your grandfather and great-grandfather before him were.

Contrary to the name, we don't kill the shifters we live near. We are charged with protecting their way of life and making sure none go rogue and take human life. We've worked side-by-side with them for centuries to keep a balance and encourage peace.

227

As much as we strive to be part of their community, you must realize that someday you may have to make the decision to go to extremes to protect them, and in some cases, put one down who has become a threat to society.

You'll know what to do when that time comes. We all have.

Be strong, my little Hunter.

I love you.

Dad

The date at the top read two years before he'd killed Mr. Cress. Before he'd decided Momma should take her away from here and never look back. Before he'd decided Samantha was supposed to forsake this lineage she'd known nothing about.

The journal smelled of aged leather, and the thin paper crackled against her fingertips. The first several pages were a collection of names and relationships. Her family tree. *Samantha Jane Young* was scrawled in black ink at the very bottom.

Next came sketches of ancient looking bears fighting men with spears in their hands. Pages and pages were filled with journal entries from different people who matched distant relatives. It was a scientific account of the migration of the bear shifters they followed.

Where they lived and for how long.

The numbers of males, females and cubs in each clan.

The figures in the first few entries numbered in the tens of thousands, and each clan had five-hundred members at least. Many of them were led by one family. Cress. But as she read the faded handwriting about wars, diseases, and battles with humans throughout history, the numbers dwindled. By the last entry, only a hundred remained, and the Hunters had scattered.

All but her father.

Dad seemed to be the last active one, as his handwriting detailed the population of Joseph. A list of alphas was written in the side margin, and he'd sketched a tree with the names of Bron and Trent, and four generations of Cress men before them.

A Hunter's duty was to stay on the outside, friendly with the clan, close with the alphas to monitor trouble before it arose for humans and bear shifters alike. They were the middle men who helped keep peace between the supernatural and human worlds.

Every word read, every page studied, she tucked the book back into its resting place beneath the hidden floorboard and replaced the carpet.

The rain had slowed to an occasional patter against the window, and she pulled her knees to her chest like it would protect her from the unknown world she'd stumbled upon.

She hadn't known it, but as a Hunter, her duty was to stay close and on the outside all at once. Instead, she'd made the mistake of falling in love with a Cress alpha.

"Smooth, fuckin' move," she muttered dryly.

Her phone chirped and she pulled it from her pocket. Another text from Reese.

Tried to check on Bron today but he's MIA. I'm at his house right now and he's not here either. Where are you? We need to talk.

Samantha hated texting, so she hit the call button and leaned her head back against the wall.

"Sam?" Reese answered.

"Yeah, it's me." Her voice sounded tired, even to her own ears. "I think I know where he is. I'll go talk to him."

"Oh, thank God. He went to your house yesterday and when he saw you'd left, he lost it. I've never seen him so…I'm glad you came back. Sam?"

"Hmm?" She was still mad, but more than that she was hurt. If Reese was looking for forgiveness right now, she didn't have it in her yet.

"I'm sorry I didn't tell you. I was under orders not to."

"I'm a Hunter, Reese. I'm supposed to know about you. None of you trusted me with this. It's not okay. Not yet."

A beat of heavy silence followed. "I know. I deserve for you to be mad, I just hate it."

"Me too." Samantha hugged her knees and closed her eyes. "I'll call you later."

"Okay," Reese said in a small voice. "Bye."

****

The old lovers' bridge was splintered and dilapidated. It no longer looked safe to hold a car's weight as it traveled over the river, but it held a man just fine. Bron leaned against the railing, looking down into the murky water below.

The rain was nothing more than a mist now, but

his black cotton T-shirt was soaked, like he'd been out here for some time. The look he slid to her was agonized as she pulled up, and he slipped a pair of sunglasses over his eyes before she was even able to cut the engine and step out of her car.

"I thought you left again," he said low as she approached. "Your suitcase was gone."

Standing beside him to look out over the water, she murmured, "You should've told me. It should've never got to a point where I found out what you are like that."

"You said they were monsters." The sunglasses hid every emotion, but his profile was rigid against the churning, stormy sky.

"What?"

"Yesterday, when Duncan and Rod flipped the cars, you saw one of them in their bear forms, and you kept calling them monsters."

"Because I didn't know a bear could flip three vehicles. I was scared, and bear shifters weren't even in the realm of possibilities for me."

"But can't you understand I didn't want you to see me like that? I didn't want you to look at me like you did when you saw me change. You were horrified. I didn't want to scare you, and I sure as shit didn't want to drag you into this life where you're always in danger. You know now, Sam. Everybody knows you know. There's no undoing this now."

"I went and visited my dad," she said as her throat tightened.

Bron pushed off the bridge railing and turned his back on her, ran his hands roughly through his hair. Then he spun and pulled her against his chest until she was enveloped in his warmth. "I couldn't tell you," he said low.

"I've hated him all this time and he was the one who saved me. I hadn't even known I was in danger." A sob wrenched from her throat.

Bear or man, she didn't care. She needed Bron to hold her and make her feel like everything was going to be okay.

"He's in that awful place because of me," she whispered.

Bron stroked her hair comfortingly. "It was his choice, and he came to terms with that a long time ago."

"He told me you visit him."

Bron sighed. "When your mom passed, he didn't

have anyone else to look forward to seeing. He helped me save you when I didn't know what to do. I didn't know it would end like that when I told him my dad's plans for you. But I don't think it could've gone any differently. It was my crazy old man, or you. Me, Trent and Tommy picked you. I go see your dad every two weeks, and I put money into his account so he can be as comfortable as possible in there. I was afraid to tell you because I could see how mad it made you to find out we talked on the phone. I was just a kid who didn't know how to save his girlfriend, and your dad did what needed to be done to protect his own. If you knew the plans my dad had for you, you wouldn't have mourned his death. He was the crazy one, not your dad. It was no great loss when he pushed Tommy's hand. He should've known better than to put a hit on a Hunter's daughter, but all he could see was what you were doing to me. He thought you made me weak."

"And do I?"

He eased back and cupped her face. "No." His tone was so steady, so sure, it was impossible not to believe him. "You make me better."

She entwined her fingers in his and kissed his

palm. Her voice was no more than a whisper when she said, "I would've loved you anyway. Bear or man, I would've loved you the same. You didn't trust me."

"I trust you, Sam. I just wanted to protect you. My clan doesn't do things like you're used to. We fight, and bleed each other because we must. Because our bears demand it. Violence and affection can look the same."

"You wouldn't hurt me."

"Never. You're too fragile. Too fragile to be exposed to any of us."

"But I'm a Hunter. I read the book about my lineage. I'm supposed to be a part of your world."

"No. You're supposed to sit on the outside, where it's safe, and only if we move to hurt humans are you supposed to get involved."

"Am I your mate?"

"Who told you about that?"

"Dillon said it. Please don't be mad at him. I just want to know what is happening between us, because it doesn't feel like it looks with other people. I can't move on, and it kills me to stay stagnant in a life away from you. What is this?"

"Yes. You're mine. The bond started when we

were nine and I was too young to know I was supposed to stop it. By the time the clan saw what was happening, it was too late."

"But you married Muriel."

She looked so small and sad reflected in his sunglasses, and she slipped her fingers out of his and reached up to remove them. His eyes were closed as she tossed them into the river below. "Don't you hide from me anymore, Bron. If I'm yours, you'll show me everything. I want all of you. The bear shit your instincts tell you to hide from me, the nightmares and shifter challenges and all of the grit that comes along with what you are. I need to know the man I love, not love a man who won't share himself with me."

His eyes opened slowly, and they couldn't pass for human if he tried. Bright silver churned in their depths, pushing away any hint of green. "I married Muriel because it was forced by the clan. After my father died, there were still others who felt he was justified in trying to take your life. Marrying Muriel was the only way I could see at the time to keep you safe. I wasn't as strong and didn't know how to fight yet, and I'd made a promise to Tommy that I would protect you no matter what. I only met her once before I married her. It was all arranged for us. I didn't tell you until the last minute because I was searching for a way out of it. She is daughter to the alpha of a small clan that lives at the base of He Devil. Our union allied our clans and made it possible for Dodger to cut you out of my life all at once. He was new to being an alpha at the time and it was the perfect solution in his mind until it became obvious my bond to you had stuck. I respected Muriel. She tried to make the best out of a marriage she didn't want either. But there was no bond between us. There was barely friendship. And now you're back here, with me, and in more danger than ever. You can't stay in Joseph. You have to leave this place."

"I can't leave here without you," she said, closing her eyes against the tears that threatened to spill.

"You won't have to," he murmured, stroking her cheek with his thumb. "I'm going with you."

"But Muriel told me what you will sacrifice if you leave."

"Fuck the consequences. I wasn't happy living here without you. And every time I think of you leaving, my animal shreds me from the inside out. I've changed eight times since yesterday. Living like that isn't an option for me."

He would give up his alpha rank and his people for her. He was declaring himself for her like she'd yearned for him to do all this time. Except now she knew what that sacrifice meant. He would brave the human world alone, and they would struggle to keep what he was a secret. She might make him happy for a little while, but he couldn't live like that for always.

He would feel caged. His animal would be stifled as he tried to pretend at normalcy for her. She could see it so clearly. Holiday celebrations and dinners with friends. Concerts and dates, and all the while he would fight his inner animal to appear normal for her.

That's not what she wanted. Not anymore.

Normal Bron didn't exist, and trying to shove him into this mold she didn't even care about was unacceptable. Man or beast, she loved all of him. His bear had fought his own people for her, and when he'd shifted, there had been no hesitancy to attack anyone who tried to hurt her.

He said she was his, but he was also hers, and she would be damned if she would stifle any part of the man she loved.

Bron's inhuman gaze sank to her lips and she smiled in invitation. "The last time we were here, you broke my heart," she said as he canted his head. "Don't do that again."

"Never. We'll leave here and I'll keep you safe. I won't be forced to choose another." His open gaze lifted to hers, as if he wanted to show her the truth of his words. "You're everything."

His strong hands found her waist and he lifted her onto the railing. He sipped her lips like he couldn't get enough of her, and she wrapped her arms around his shoulders. From up here, she was level with his glorious eyes. They didn't scare her now. They were a part of himself he was finally letting her see, and happiness bloomed within her.

"I want to jump," she murmured, pulling back by inches. "I want to do this over. Do it right this time."

A slow smile spread across his face and she touched the corner of his mouth with her fingertip just to feel the curve there. He pulled the hem of her blue cotton shirt until she was free of it, and they laughed as they kicked out of their jeans.

It was freezing out here, but she didn't care. Not when the open happiness on Bron's face made her feel so warm inside. With ease, he lifted her to the railing by her waist and steadied her, then followed her up. Standing there together, over the gentle river rapids, hand in hand, he stared at her with such adoration.

"You ready?" he asked.

"Ready."

Samantha shrieked as they jumped and sailed downward. The cold water was a shock to her system, and she kicked her way to the surface and gasped as the frigid waves lapped at her bare skin.

The water was high and she couldn't touch the bottom until they neared the sandy beach.

"Come on." Bron led her from the beach and lifted her into his arms when she stumbled on a river rock. "I want to show you something."

She wanted to protest on account of it being roughly the temperature of a glacier right now, but Bron was like a furnace against her skin. As waves of gooseflesh prickled her arms, his skin stayed smooth and warm. He tucked her against his chest tighter as he stepped around trees and through brush.

Her mouth fell open as he set her down in a grove of red maples. The storm must have knocked their leaves loose, because the ground was covered in crimson. She sent a wide-eyed glance at Bron over her shoulder, and stepped into the untouched forest. As far as she could see was red so bright, it stunned her. And all around her, leaves rained down in a never-ending shower. She turned in a slow circle and plucked one from the air.

Bron crouched down, his dark boxers clinging to him as he watched her with bright eyes. "You're so beautiful."

Her cheeks flushed warmly under his attention. "So are you."

"Come here." His cocky smile said he knew she'd do as he said.

"Bossy," she teased as she straddled his lap.

He laughed a booming sound that echoed through the autumn woods and leaned back on his locked elbows. "If that's the worst name you have for me after all I've put you through, I'm okay with that."

"The Hunter's notebook said you can't mate with humans," she blurted out.

"We can't breed with them." His voice dipped low. "I can't get you with child no matter how much I want to."

Her heart ached at the sadness on his face. "You want babies?"

"Yes. I've always wanted a couple of cubs running around. That life isn't meant for me and you though. You'll have to be happy with just me."

Leaning forward, she kissed him sweetly. "Are you sure I'm worth all of this. Giving up your people and your life here. Giving up your position in your clan and the possibility of a family. Are you sure you want to leave with me?"

"Yes," he said, void of hesitation. "That's the decision I should have made six years ago, when I was given the ultimatum. I think I would've, if I thought you'd be safe with me."

"I feel safe with you now."

A deep rumble of content sounded from his chest, and she pressed her hand against the vibration and smiled. She knew what that meant now. Her bear was in there, and happy with her. She brushed her lips right above his heart, and he dropped his chin back as she trailed her lips to his throat.

Now she could place the subtle scent of animal that had always clung to his skin. Between them, his cock grew thick and hard, and she rocked against him. Straightening his spine, Bron cupped the side of her face and ran his thumb down her cold cheek, warming it with his touch. Canting his head, he pulled her toward him and pressed his tongue gently past her lips.

Gripping his hair, she bit his lip and pulled his head back until the thick muscles in his neck strained. "Don't ever lie to me again. From here on, it's you and me. I can handle your secrets."

Moving her panties to the side, he lifted her by the waist and settled her over his cock slowly. A huff of air brushed past her lips as she took all of him.

"I swear I won't lie to you again." His arms wrapped around her back and he settled her more firmly onto him, and he drew one of her nipples, beaded tight against the cold air, into his mouth.

She moaned at the contrast of his soft lips and gently grazing teeth. Arching her hips, she pulled back by inches, and rammed back down, breasts bobbing with her motion.

He curled against her, gripped her back. "Fuuuck," he said in a shaky whisper.

Every sway of her hips made him tense, and when he pulled his inhuman gaze to hers, she knew she had him. He looked desperate for her, eyebrows drawn up in awe, heart hammering against his sternum where her palm rested, and she wanted to be closer. Wanted to burrow against and inside of him and never let go. They'd been apart for too long and it had nearly broken her, but here in his arms, she felt whole again.

Her legs flexed again as she rose and fell, and his fingers dug into her back like he was on the edge. She reveled in having such an effect on someone so strong.

"Sam," he gritted out. His voice sounded so raw and needy, and she pulled a long stroke again.

"You can't come when we go this slow. I remember," she whispered, and tugged his earlobe into her mouth, teasing.

He ground out a desperate sound, and bucked his hips against her. It was enough to send her over, and her insides quaked with ecstasy. Tossing back her head, she yelled out as he pressed into her, and her insides clenched around his shaft. Pleasure rolled through her as thunder sounded in the distance.

Pattering rain dropped from the sky and splashed onto her face and breasts, but it only heightened the sensation. Cold water, cool breeze, damp from the swim, and Bron, so warm and alive against her. His skin pressing inside of her as he rocked fiercely. He felt so good buried in her, filling her.

He deserved to be rewarded for his patience. Easing back, she watched his expression change from confused to triumphant as she turned around and splayed on hands and knees. With a wicked smile over her shoulder, she arched her back until her slick folds were angled toward him.

His eyes were so bright, so ravenous as he raked his gaze over her. Mounting her, he covered her back with his body and slid into her sex again. Slow, powerful thrusts gave way to shorter ones, and her breath quickened as the tension grew.

His cock seemed to grow harder and thicker the more he slammed into her and she could tell the moment his animal took over. His growl turned feral and his voice gravelly as he groaned her name. He straightened and grabbed her waist with both hands, pulling her back against him with every flex of his hips.

She shattered again, screaming his name as the first shot of warmth filled her.

Bron's roar was long, and shook the red maple trees around them.

And she'd never loved him more than in this moment, when he finally gave her both sides of him.

FOURTEEN

With shaking fingers, Samantha pulled Muriel's phone number from her pocket and keyed it into her cell. She was sitting in front of the only gas station in town, where she had been trying to convince herself to make the call for the last ten minutes.

Time was running out. Bron wanted to leave tonight, and this was the only chance she'd get to make things right. Or as right as things could get for a man like Bron.

She hadn't been able to stop thinking about Muriel's offer. It was a constant *what if* in her mind, and the more she realized what Bron would really be giving up, the more her potential sacrifice seemed justified.

Did she want to become like Bron, and go through all the pain and secrecy his life required? Absolutely not. But whether she wanted to be a part of this or not, her life was tethered to him now. And if she was a shifter like him, no one could oppose their pairing. He could stay here among his people, and if she lived through the transition, he could lead the remaining bear shifters of Hells Canyon, like he was supposed to.

He was made to lead them. It was so painfully clear that she was disrupting his fate, and she refused to do that anymore.

Muriel said turning would hurt, and that there would be risk, but Samantha believed that she would do her best to turn her. She believed Muriel when she admitted Samantha was her ticket to happiness. Bron had to move on for her to find a new mate, and she would do her best to keep Samantha alive through the change.

This was her compromise. Because of all the sacrifices Bron had made to keep her safe, the risk was worth it.

Just thinking about the repercussions of this decision made her hands shake even harder. Maybe if she lived and became a bear, she would be stronger. Perhaps she could be the mate Bron deserved to have by his side.

"Hello?" Muriel said on the other line.

"It's me. Samantha. I've thought about your offer."

"And?" she asked. Was that hope Samantha heard in her tone?

"And I want to try. For Bron. He deserves it."

"I'll text you my address. Does he know of your decision?"

"No."

"Best hurry then, little future bear. Your new mate is a tracker."

The text came through fine and Samantha weaved through the streets to the other side of town. She lost the GPS signal on a one lane dirt road that led toward the Seven Devils, but a mailbox read Muriel Marsden beside a muddy turnoff. It seemed Muriel liked to live out in the wilderness too. Was that a bear shifter thing, wanting to live outside of human society? Perhaps her new instincts would demand the same if she survived tonight.

She should've told Bron a better goodbye, but if she had, he would've been suspicious, and she

needed him to keep packing up his house while she
ran her secret errand. If he knew what she was about
to attempt to do, he would've brought hell on earth to
stop her. He wouldn't approve of the risk, even if it
was her decision to make.

A cabin much smaller than Bron's stood between
two giant pines. Every window was lit, and homey
looking. Thunder rumbled as she stepped out of the
car and sprinted up the sidewalk, and rain pounded
down against her shoulders in punishing waves.

Muriel waited at the front door and ushered her
inside. The cabin was warm, and Muriel seemed to be
a collector of old, worn-in furniture. Nothing matched
but everything seemed to go together in a way that
Samantha could never pull off. As much as she
wished she had better taste, her decorating sense
tended to veer toward college dorm room chic.

"I like your place," she said nervously.

"Thanks. Most of it I inherited from my mom."
Muriel led her into a room that had rows of dried
plants hanging upside down in the window. One wall
was covered with pages of hastily printed notes and
sketches of plants and animals. The room smelled
strongly of spices and something chemical. She

picked up a small jelly jar and shook the contents. "I'm going to poison you."

"Wait," Samantha said, arching her eyebrows high. "What?"

"Your vitals have to be moving in slow motion for this to work. To give the bear a chance to take over, you'll have to be on the brink of death when you're given the toxin that will turn you. Your heart rate will slow to almost nothing, and in that moment, that's when you need to change."

"And if I'm unable?"

"Once you take this, there is no going back. You turn or you die. I've put as much help in here as I can give. You'll be able to survive on less everything. Less oxygen, less blood pumping through your veins. But once this slips past your lips, there is no changing your mind."

"What are my odds of survival?"

"I don't like doing odds. It's better to think positive—that you will make it through this. But you should know, there is a chance this won't work."

Samantha sank heavily into a chair in the corner of the room. This was a terrible risk to take when she'd just found Bron again.

"Listen," Muriel said, kneeling down in front of her. "If you think you and Bron can find happiness outside of Joseph, then don't do this. I'll do everything in my power to get you through the transition, but we stopped turning humans decades ago because of the risk. It got to where none of you survived at all."

"What makes you think I will be different?"

"Because the knowledge has been passed down from generation to generation in my family. I was raised with medicine women who kept these secrets close to their hearts. And I know what the others were doing wrong."

"What?"

"They were trying to turn grizzlies for war. You can't put a dominant animal like that in a human and expect the human side to survive. You have to be born with a grizzly. What kind would you like to be?"

"What kind of bear?"

"Black bear is most common, but you can choose and Andean or Sun bear as well. They're smaller, less volatile, and you'll have a better shot at living with one of them inside of you."

"So I just...pick a bear like out of a catalogue?"

"I've collected the toxins from my clan. I have a

vial of each."

"Are Andean bears the ones with the white faces?"

Muriel nodded. "Not many of those left. If you survive, you would be one of three."

This wasn't like picking which earrings to get her ears pierced with. Samantha was picking which freaking bear to put inside of herself. She closed her eyes and wished Reese was here. She should've said a proper goodbye to her, too.

She imagined Bron never having the opportunity to track down who killed his brother and what that would do to him. She imagined living outside of Joseph as Bron withered without his people. Visions of his clan dying out because they didn't have a strong enough leader pulled at her heart and she took the jelly jar from Muriel's hands.

"Save me," she said, then tipped the rim to her mouth before she could change her mind.

The liquid scorched heat down her throat and was bitter against her tongue. Gulping, she pressed the back of her hand over her lips so she wouldn't gag.

Her vision blurred, doubled, then focused again

as she watched Muriel fill a syringe. The woman's green eyes flicked to her and back to the needle. She looked as nervous as Samantha felt. If she died in here tonight, Muriel would have to live with that on her conscience.

Samantha hoped she lived for the both of them.

Swaying, she gasped for breath that seemed to suddenly congeal in her lungs. She was going to suffocate! Falling from the chair, she crawled aimlessly as Muriel dropped beside her. The prick of pain in her arm and the burning tendrils that stretched up to her shoulder was secondary to her throat closing.

No bear could survive if her body couldn't breathe.

Panic seized her as her elbows locked. Wheezing, she went rigid as Muriel lifted her and rushed her outside. She'd been so stupid! What had made her think she was stronger than the other humans the shifters had tried to turn?

Bron, Bron, Bron.

She wouldn't ever see him again. Wouldn't touch him or kiss him or feel his warmth. She would never share his secrets and see the smile he saved only for her. The wrong decision had been made, and now she would die here in a stranger's arms.

Something big pulsed within her. Raw power crashed against her bones and made her body arch back with the discomfort of the humming vibration. She wanted to scream, but a snarl of agony ripped from her throat instead.

She had to breathe.

"Samantha, you have to change. You'll be fine as long as you can change. You'll feel better. Do you feel her in you?"

With short panting breaths and wide eyes, Samantha nodded. Rain splashed against her cheeks as Muriel lay her crumpled body on the damp grass.

"Close your eyes and let her have your body," Muriel whispered. She looked so scared in the light from the window.

Samantha's heart was glugging against her sternum, slowing, and her arms felt heavy as if they were encased in cement. Closing her eyes, she tried to force the animal out. The humming came closer to the surface, and excruciating pain rippled down her spine.

Panicked and delirious, she fought and struggled

against what was happening to her.

Convulsing, her body was wracked with hacking coughs. She tasted iron.

Muriel's green eyes went round.

"Bron," Samantha whispered.

Muriel pulled a cell phone from the back pocket of her jeans and hit a speed dial number. "Bron?" she asked. Her voice sounded like she was about to cry. "It's Samantha. Come to my house right now."

"What's happened?" he asked. The sound of his voice was amplified and pounded against Samantha's ears. She screamed and clamped her hands over her them.

"I tried to change her," Muriel said with a sob. "I'm sorry!"

The line went dead.

"Samantha, listen, honey, you have to change." Muriel's voice sounded desperate. "There's no choice for you now. You have to let that bear out before you become too weak. Just let her out and you'll feel okay again."

Another spasming cough and Muriel leaned her forward as Samantha wretched. She'd hoped to rid her body of the poison, but her body seemed bound and determined to keep it all inside.

Another pulse of power raged through her, and Samantha gritted her teeth as her spine felt like it was splitting in two. Her arms were so heavy as she rolled over and crawled through the mud. Gasping, she clutched wet tufts of grass as another feral growl ripped through her.

"That's it, Samantha. Relax and let it happen."

But no matter how hard she tried to give the beast her body, whatever was supposed to happen just didn't. And now it was hard to move. Minutes felt like hours and when she looked down at her hands to figure out where the warmth was coming from, red spattered across her knuckles. It was dripping from her mouth.

That scared her more than anything. She was on borrowed time, and even if she could breathe a little easier now with the effects of the poison slowing everything down, and even if her heart wasn't racing anymore, it was getting harder to move and her vision was blurring around the edges.

Crunching gravel, boots sloshing through the mud, the rain looked so beautiful in front of the headlights of Bron's truck.

Yelling.

Someone was crying but they sounded far away.

Her neck arched back as Bron's strong hands positioned under her shoulder blades.

She tried to smile.

He looked so scared.

"She needs to change!" Muriel sobbed. Where was she? Samantha wished she could tell her it was all right so she wouldn't live for always with the guilt of her death on her conscience.

Silver, inhuman eyes caressed her skin before Bron clutched her against him. He was so warm and she was so damned cold.

"What have you done?" he whispered brokenly. Easing back, he brushed the wet hair from her face and tried in vain to wipe the red from her chin. His hands were covered in the stuff as she gasped for life.

Samantha couldn't see much beyond Bron. The lights from his truck surrounded his head with light. "You're beautiful," she rasped.

"Change with me, Sam." His voice cracked. "My Sam. Do you want to change together?"

Words had left her. Burning lungs wouldn't let her draw enough breath to push past her vocal cords.

Her heart beat so slowly in her ear, and he pressed his fingers against her pulse.

Weakly, she dipped her chin in answer. The end was coming, but she didn't want to disappoint him. Not when this is what would be seared into his mind for the rest of his life. She wanted him to know she tried until the end.

"Change!" he bellowed into the woods. The crack of power in his voice caressed the hum inside of her.

When she turned her head, Muriel, Reese and Dillon were all there, hovering near the tree line. Reese was soaking wet and sobbing, but she pulled her shirt over her head and dropped to all fours with the others. Squinting, Samantha tried to hold onto their blurred forms as they turned into monstrous bears.

"Watch me, love. Change with me, please. Samantha," Bron whispered as he lowered his forehead to hers. "I need you."

A burst of pops sounded and Bron gritted his teeth as his face elongated. Rearing up, an enormous grizzly burst from him and he stood over her, great paws on either side of her face as he stared at her with such determination. His chest heaved as he inhaled, and tipping his head back, he roared.

The sound filled her veins, and rushed her stuttering heartbeat. The hum inside her grew more urgent and she braced against the ground as her body shattered. The illumination of the headlights was too bright, and Samantha closed her eyes against the ringing pain.

He was calling to her. Calling her bear from deep within her. A hundred pops cracked up her spine, and each was accompanied by unimaginable pain. She was being shot and electrified and drowned all at once.

Her scream filled the clearing, and when she dragged air into her lungs to do it again, the roar that bellowed from her throat was a direct answer to Bron's.

There *she* was—the animal that was now a part of her.

The bear was desperate and scared and clawing her way out of Samantha's body. Tears fled the corners of her eyes as her face broke and her teeth curved and stretched down. Black, six-inch long claws pushed through her finger tips as her hands transformed into massive, ebony-black furred paws.

One final wave of pain stretched from her snout to her hind legs and disappeared as if she'd never been hurt at all. She stood stunned and swaying, uncertain on legs she didn't yet know how to command. The sick feeling the poison had left fizzled away in her stomach until she felt no discomfort at all. Only weakness and exhaustion.

Bron stood in shadow near his truck, his profile to her, frozen in place like he couldn't understand how she'd come to be here. She moved to join him, desperate for his reassurance, but fell forward onto the wet grass with a grunt.

He was there in an instant, and his oversized nose pressed against the fur at her neck, inhaling deeply as the soft rumble she recognized so well rattled from his throat.

She was alive.

Relief washed through her, making her feel unbalanced as her human emotions clashed against the confusion of being in a body that was *other*. Bron raked her closer to him with his oversized paw, and a soft whimper wrenched from her throat as the relief of his touch threatened to drown her with happiness.

Another paw touched her back, and another as

the other bears gathered near and pressed against her. Their warmth seeped through the coldness that had taken her in the throes of that awful pain, and soft grunts filled the night as her clan mates familiarized themselves with her new form. Reese lay beside her and sighed heavily, and Dillon pressed a paw on her back as he watched the road like he was standing sentinel.

And Bron, covered in scars of battles she knew nothing about yet, watching her with such pride in his soft eyes, nuzzled her face until she huffed a laugh deep in her throat.

She'd chosen right. In this moment, as her mate stood protectively over her, she could see the choice was always supposed to be this.

She loved him more than anything.

After everything they'd been through and given up, she and Bron deserved to be happy.

And now they could be.

EPILOGUE

"Okay," Bron murmured. "Open your eyes."

Samantha pulled her hands away from her face and gasped. Dillon, Reese and Bron had been working on the outside of the house from sunup until now, while she'd been ordered to stay inside and finish up the last touches on the interior of the house.

The wooden plank walls of the house had been replaced and painted dark brown with white trim. The porch swing drifted easily in the breeze and had been newly whitewashed to match the railing. The overgrown weeds had been mowed, and the front flower bed was lined with trimmed shrubs and autumn mums in yellows and rusty reds.

A young red maple had been planted in the yard.

"It's perfect," she breathed.

"I was thinking we could keep it," Bron said. "When you're ready, I want you in the cabin with me, but your dad will get out in a few years and we could give him his old house. Before you say no, you should know that I aim to help him transition back. That was always the plan."

She shook her head in disbelief that such an honorable man was hers. "Why would I say no? I think it would suit him. And he'll be close to the clan again, like he's supposed to be."

The smile that stretched Bron's face was so full of adoration, she melted into the side of him, under the warm protection of his arm. "*Our* clan," he said softly.

Tonight they would tell Dodger and the rest of the Hells Canyon shifters what she had become. Bron had called a meeting, and she would show them that she belonged in Joseph, a member of this clan and a part of this community.

Hunter and bear, the first of her kind, and one of the last Andean shifters in the world, she would walk through life beside the man who held her heart.

Bron had vowed to find Trent's murderer, and she would be there when he did. And she would support him as he took his place as alpha. The future was still uncertain, but whatever destiny had in store for them, she would take life as it came and appreciate every day with him as the gift it was.

Her breath shook and her eyes burned with tears she quickly dashed away with the back of her hand. She'd worked so hard to get to this moment.

Reese clutched her other hand, and Dillon studied the house they'd fixed together with such pride. This was what fate had in mind when she'd bonded with Bron all those years ago. She'd been mistaken when she'd thought the path her life was supposed to take had been broken. She was supposed to be with the people she loved the most, right here—standing with her clan, in the shadow of the Seven Devils Mountains.

Bron looked down at her, his eyebrows furrowed as if her tears worried him.

"Thank you," she whispered, grateful for all the happiness he'd brought into her life. Thankful that he'd finally let her in.

He ran the pad of his thumb across her cheek where the moisture of her tears had been. Leaning down, his lips curved into an irresistible smile just before he pressed them to hers.

This had always been her home. She'd just taken the long way getting back to it.

And as the evening shadows stretched across the yard, and the cicadas began their familiar song in the woods beyond, she was taken with the beauty of her life.

She'd had to die and come back to appreciate the importance of this place.

She'd had to heed the call of her bear.

Want more of these characters?

Call of the Bear is the first book in the Hells Canyon Shifters series.

For more of these characters, check out these other books from T. S. Joyce.

Fealty of the Bear
(Hells Canyon Shifters, Book 2)

Avenge the Bear
(Hells Canyon Shifters, Book 3)

Claim the Bear
(Hells Canyon Shifters, Book 4)

Heart of the Bear
(Hells Canyon Shifters, Book 5)

About the Author

T.S. Joyce is devoted to bringing hot shifter romances to readers. Hungry alpha males are her calling card, and the wilder the men, the more she'll make them pour their hearts out. She werebear swears there'll be no swooning heroines in her books. It takes tough-as-nails women to handle her shifters.

She lives in a tiny town, outside of a tiny city, and devotes her life to writing big stories. Foodie, wolf whisperer, ninja, thief of tiny bottles of awesome smelling hotel shampoo, nap connoisseur, movie fanatic, and zombie slayer, and most of this bio is true.

Bear Shifters? Check

Smoldering Alpha Hotness? Double Check

Sexy Scenes? Fasten up your girdles, ladies and gents, it's gonna to be a wild ride.

For more information on T. S. Joyce's work,
visit her website at
www.tsjoyce.com

Printed in Great Britain
by Amazon